FABLED BEAST CHRONICLES

Wolf Notes
and
Other Musical Mishaps

LARI DON

 Kelpies

Kelpies is an imprint of Floris Books

First published in 2009 by Floris Books
This new edition published in 2014

The publisher acknowledges subsidy from Creative
Scotland towards the publication of this volume

Cover font designed by Juan Casco
www.juancasco.net

 This book is also available
as an eBook

MIX
Paper from
responsible sources
FSC® C117931
www.fsc.org
FSC

British Library CIP Data available
ISBN 978-178250-138-1
Printed in Great Britain
by DS Smith Print Solutions, Glasgow

To Mirren and Gowan,
who wanted fangs this time,
and to Colin, who found his
first wolf note

Chapter 1

Helen was woken in the unfamiliar bed by an almost familiar sound.

Clip clop clip "shhhhh!"

She sat up.

Clip clop clip crash!

She pushed the duvet aside and slid her feet down to the polished floorboards.

She wasn't in her own bedroom, so she moved carefully in the dark. Her outstretched fingers touched the wardrobe door. She didn't need her fleece or her fiddle case, so she moved to her left, found the bedroom door and eased it open.

She couldn't hear anything. No hoof beats. No whispers. No crashes. Had she imagined the noise? Had she been dreaming?

Then she heard it again.

Clip clop clip clop. And a sob.

The sound was coming from downstairs. That made sense. No hoofed beast could climb the narrow staircase. Helen crept towards the top of the stairs. She didn't want to wake the other summer school students on their first night in the lodge; she didn't want to alarm the intruder below.

She started down the stairs, one steep step at a time. Turning a sharp corner, she moved into a blur of yellow light. She paused, listening.

The scrape of a hoof? Breathing? The scrape of something larger. A brief mutter.

What was going on?

There was no one in the corridor below her; the kitchen and the bathroom on the left were both dark. The light was coming from the doorway to the right of the stairs, from the living room that was being used as a rehearsal room. She tiptoed down to the bottom and peered slowly round the door.

Now she could see as well as hear the hooves on the wooden floor. They were stepping round a fallen bookcase. Under the bookcase, she saw a girl. No. A dog. No. A girl. No! A wolf!

Helen gasped, the boy high above the hooves

turned, and past his long legs she saw she'd been mistaken. Trapped under the bookcase was a girl. Definitely a girl.

Helen walked up to the boy with the dark red hair and the chestnut horse's body, whispering, "Hello, Yann."

"Healer's child!" The centaur's voice was sharp with surprise.

She glanced at the pale girl by his hooves. "Does your friend need my help?"

Rather than waiting for an answer, Helen slid her hands under one side of the bookcase. The centaur leant down as low as he could and grasped the other side. On his whispered count of three, they heaved the bookcase off the girl. She groaned, but didn't move.

They propped the empty bookcase between a flowery armchair and the wall, then started lifting books and sheet music off the girl.

The bookcase had been filled with printed music, but metronomes and music stands had also been piled onto its deep middle shelves.

After Helen and Yann had shifted the loose paper, they realized that a metal joint from a music stand had stabbed the girl in the upper arm.

"Yann, should I call a doctor, or does your friend distrust humans as much as you do?" Helen asked gently.

Yann grimaced. "If *you* could heal her, we would be grateful."

Helen sighed and climbed back up to the door nearest the top of the stairs. She put her bedroom light on then opened her wardrobe. She'd wedged her violin case on the highest shelf and behind it she'd hidden an old green rucksack. She didn't know why she'd brought the rucksack to Dorry Shee, but now she was glad she had.

Helen crept downstairs again and saw Yann bent over the girl. She was wearing grey fleecy trousers and vest, with no obvious buttons, zips or Velcro. Her long hair was silver blonde, a colour that would look almost grey on someone older. Her eyes were glistening gold. When she saw Helen staring at her, she bared her teeth in a growl, or possibly an attempt at a smile through the pain.

Helen knelt beside her. "I'm going to pull the metal out of your arm, then cover the wound, if you'll let me."

The girl looked up at Yann, who smiled reassuringly.

Helen tied back her curly dark hair, then examined the arm. It was slim, but strongly muscled. Perhaps the girl was a violinist! Then Helen noticed the girl's hands. Those long nails would be no use for fingering strings.

The metal spike had penetrated the girl's skin, but hadn't cut too deeply into her arm.

"Yann, hold her tight. This might hurt."

Yann's front legs knelt on the floor and he grasped the girl's shoulders. Helen put one hand on the girl's left elbow and with the other she steadily pulled the length of metal out of the girl's arm. The girl whimpered, once.

The wound started to overflow with blood. Helen opened the rucksack, shaking her head at her lack of planning. She should have taken all the necessary equipment out of the first aid kit before she began. Despite all the lambing, run-over dogs and other veterinary expeditions she had helped her mum with this spring and summer, she was still a beginner at first aid.

She stemmed the bleeding with sterile swabs, then lifted the arm high, to slow the flow. "Hold it up for a minute, then I'll bandage it."

She kept her hand curled round the girl's elbow to take the arm's weight, then finally looked straight at Yann.

"What are *you* doing here?" they both whispered at once.

There was a moment's silence. Then they both spoke again.

"What are …?"

Helen sighed. Yann scowled.

"You first," offered Helen.

"Me first," demanded Yann.

She grinned. He cleared his throat. "Your home in Clovenshaws is many miles away, to the south and east of these forests. What are you doing here?"

"I'm here for the music summer school; the one I was auditioning for when we met last winter. Professor Greenhill has rented the lodge for our school and, at the end of the week, we'll be performing nearby for a specially invited audience. You live miles from here too, Yann. Why are you here? Why have you and your friend broken into our rehearsal room?"

"I can't tell you why we are here, just that you must leave. This is not a safe place for human children, especially ones so skilled in music. You must go. Now!"

"You've got to be kidding!" Helen's whisper cracked into a yell. She lowered her voice, but her shock still showed through. "I've worked incredibly hard to be chosen for this school. I've been practising for months to make sure I'm the best fiddler here. I'm not leaving until I've performed at Professor Greenhill's concert! And I won't have you and your friends interfering!"

"You must forget your musical ambitions and this Professor; you must return to the safety of your home and your mother."

"My mother! Whose help you begged last year, then had to settle for my help because she wouldn't have believed you existed? You needed me then, and I think you need me now. What's going on, Yann?"

The girl on the floor croaked, "Don't you dare tell her!"

"I won't tell her, my friend. I will simply say, healer's child, that you must leave Dorry Shee as soon as you can."

"No! Don't get between me and my music, Yann." Helen leant over the head of the bleeding girl, jabbing her finger at Yann's bare chest. "Once I've fixed up your girlfriend, you two can go away and stay away. Don't bring your chaos and quests anywhere near my midsummer music. We can meet after the concert; you can tell me about your latest big adventure then …"

The girl between them said softly, "How do you know this human child, Yann? Did you know she was here? Is that why you wouldn't let my brothers howl tonight; why you wanted me to be tame, just ripping drums and biting strings, rather than scaring the sleepers themselves?"

Helen twisted round to look at the shelves of instruments under the window. Two African djembes had rolled onto the floor, their drum skins torn open.

"Did you slash those drums?" Helen snapped.

The girl ignored her. "Who is this human, Yann, who

speaks to you as if you were her friend and to me as if I were her dog?"

Yann said in a formal voice, "Let me introduce you. This is Helen Strang, the healer's daughter, who helped me and my friends when we fought the Master of the Maze last winter. She healed my leg, gave Sapphire back her sight, saved Lavender's life and answered many riddles. She is a friend to fabled beasts."

He gestured at the girl on the floor. "This is Sylvie …"

"Don't tell her who I am!"

Yann smiled. "This is Sylvie Hunt, a shy friend of mine. I'm helping her defend the fabled beasts' territory in the West Highlands. But you won't be able to help us, healer's child, as your presence – and your music – will aid our enemies. So you must go."

"No! I'm not leaving until after the midsummer concert."

"You are leaving now, girl." Yann's voice was harsh. "Or we will drive you away."

"Is that what you were doing tonight? Trying to drive me away? Yann! How dare you?"

Sylvie moaned, her upraised arm sagging in Helen's grasp.

"Sorry!" said Helen. "I'll bandage you right now."

Asking Sylvie to sit up and Yann to support the arm, she pulled antiseptic and bandages out of the rucksack.

The girl flinched at the chemical sting as Helen disinfected the wound. Then Helen bandaged the arm quickly and neatly, but kept questioning the centaur. "Don't you know how much this summer school means to me?"

"I didn't know your summer school was here! When

13

you told us you had won an apprenticeship with your bards, I thought it would be in a town or city, not out in the wild lands!" He shrugged. "So I didn't pay any attention to where or when it was."

"Why is this place so dangerous? Is the Master of the Maze here?"

"No, he has returned to his old labyrinth to heal his wounds and grow his hair. But here is a greater danger for a human child than even the Master. We can't tell you any more, as knowledge can draw humans towards the danger. I can only ask you to leave. Please, Helen."

Yann had never called Helen by her name before, not to her face.

"Please go home, Helen."

She acknowledged the offer of deeper friendship with a smile. "Thank you for caring about my safety, Yann. But my week at this summer school isn't about safety, or even about friendship. It's about music. This is a once in a lifetime chance to play the greatest music, with the greatest musicians. I'm not running away."

The girl on the floor laughed.

"They've enchanted her already! 'A once in a lifetime chance!'" she repeated sarcastically. "It would be a lifetime! Human girl, listen to your friend. If his gentle persuasion doesn't work, my brothers won't be so soft."

This time, she did growl.

Helen laid the bandaged arm in the girl's lap and looked at her thin face.

"What *are* you?" Helen asked bluntly.

"I'm Sylvie. Yann told you."

"He told me *who* you are. Hello, Sylvie. Nice to meet

you, Sylvie. Now *what* are you? And why are you trying to drive me away?"

"Do you really want to know?" The girl's yellow eyes narrowed, her lips drew back and her long teeth gleamed white in the light from the lacy lampshade above.

"Do you *really* want to know?"

Helen felt the hairs on the back of her neck bristle.

Chapter 2

"Don't scare her, Sylvie!" Yann whispered urgently. "Perhaps we *should* explain what's going on. Helen's very calm and sensible, for a human. If we trust her with our story, she'll understand and leave."

Helen didn't feel calm and sensible. She felt nervous. Nervous of the girl in front of her. Nervous about waking the students upstairs. Nervous about losing her chance to play in the best youth concert in Scotland for years.

Anyway, calm and sensible were boring. She was an *artiste* now. That's what Professor Greenhill had said last night when they arrived.

So she stood up, stretching and saying recklessly, "You don't have to protect me, Yann. If your friend wants to scare me, let her try!"

"She's met some fabled beasts, has she?" Sylvie looked at Yann. "She thinks we're all friendly and gentle and *vegetarian*, does she?"

Yann said, "No! Don't!"

But Sylvie grinned at Helen, then vanished. She flickered in and out of sight, like lamp-posts passing a fast car window.

She was a grey dog. She was a girl in a fur coat. She was a skinny dog. She was a girl again, breathing hard. Finally, she was a dog. And she stayed a dog. No. Helen kept making that mistake. She wasn't a dog. She was a wolf.

Sylvie was a wolf.

And the bandage Helen had got just right, to show Yann her improved first aid skills, was lying bloodstained on the floor. It had slipped off the wolf's slim leg. The wound was bleeding again.

Helen swallowed, then said, "Oh dear. I'll have to put another bandage on. Are you going to be a wolf for the rest of the night, or a girl? Just so I know what size of bandage I need."

The wolf's ears jutted upwards and she snarled, showing her curved white teeth and tense pink tongue. As her top lip curled up, long dark creases ran down her snout, from between her diamond yellow eyes to her sharp black nose. A nose that was pointing straight at Helen's bare throat.

Resisting the temptation to hide behind Yann, Helen leant down to pick up the bandage. Then she stood still, right in front of the wolf, close enough to see Sylvie's ribcage move under her silvery fur.

Yann laughed proudly. "She doesn't scare easily, does she? Not all humans are scared of wolves."

Helen picked up the rucksack, thinking: actually, most humans *are* scared of wolves, but it's wiser not to let the wolf know that.

She forced her shaking fingers to rip open more swabs and tried to smile. "So, Sylvie, am I bandaging a wolf's leg, or a girl's arm? If you keep changing shape, I'll run out of bandages."

The wolf snarled again.

"I understand you better when you're a girl. If you change back, I promise I'll listen to your reasons for wanting me to leave. But if you stay a wolf, with all that fur harbouring dirt, I'll have to use an even *stronger* antiseptic." She pulled a bottle of violent blue liquid out of the rucksack. It wasn't an antiseptic, but Helen hoped Sylvie wouldn't realize that.

Sylvie whimpered. Yann laughed again.

The wolf flickered into a girl. Sylvie crouched on the floor, her hair tangled over her face, her bare arm sliding with blood.

Helen wiped the blood away, used a gentle antiseptic to clean the arm, then re-bandaged the wound. Afterwards, she busied herself repacking the first aid kit and sealing bloody swabs and bandages in a bag, while Yann and Sylvie glowered at each other.

Then Helen tried to shove the loose sheet music under the couch, to give Yann more room on the floorboards, but the dusty space was full of jigsaws and plastic animals. Helen guessed the toys belonged to the family that owned the lodge; perhaps kept here to amuse the kids while their parents renovated this wing.

She dumped the papers on top of the couch instead

and perched on one of its arms. "Will someone please tell me what's going on?"

Sylvie pointed at Yann. "He's the storyteller."

The centaur shook his head. "She healed you. You owe her your story. If you tell it right, she might even help you."

Sylvie growled her disagreement. "She can't help. If she goes near them, they'll win! Anyway, I know whose side she'll take."

"How do you know whose side I'll take?" Helen asked. "Let me make up my own mind when I've heard the story."

Sylvie sat on the other arm of the couch. "I know you were afraid of me." She leant closer. "I could smell your fear, but you did well to hide it. So I'll tell you the story of our summer battle.

"We of the wolf people have lived in these forests ..."

"Wolf people?" Helen interrupted. "Do you mean werewolves?"

Sylvie snapped at Yann, "Haven't you taught her how to listen to a story?"

Helen shrugged. "Sorry, but I like to know *who* is telling the story, before I decide how to hear it. What are you, Sylvie?"

"I am one of the wolf people, not a werewolf from your silly moonlit stories. We are an ancient tribe, not an accident of biting. We are completely in control of our shape-changing ..."

Yann snorted. "Unless you're trapped under a bookcase!"

"We are not at the beck and call of the moon, so are more powerful than the sea. We hunt as wolves, but learn as men and women, so have lasted hidden in the forests longer than our permanent wolf cousins. But now our forests and hunting grounds are under threat."

"From people? From this summer school?" Helen frowned. "We're only here for a few days! Or are you worried about more people staying at the lodge once it's finished?"

"Hidden in the trees, we've always outwitted anyone staying at this lodge," Sylvie sneered. "No, we are under threat from older forest folk. These forests, so long cut down, are growing larger again. Humans are planting trees and reintroducing old species to make the wilderness wild again.

"Now some of the wild ones have decided to reintroduce themselves.

"Those of us who never left are good at staying hidden, avoiding the attention of humans. But those who're coming back are not used to the modern world. They will return to the old ways that the rest of us live without. They will bring the wrath of humans down on us all.

"Even worse, they are planning to live on *our* land! Land we have hunted and guarded for centuries. This forest of Dorry Shee is where the young wolves hunt, the territory where we build our skills and hierarchy. They will hunt our deer with horns and hounds. They will scare away our prey and draw humans here. The wolf people will have to skulk in hedgerows and stony glens. We'll have to eat hedgehogs and squirrels, with men hunting us ... and nowhere to hide.

"We must not let them come back!"

"Who mustn't come back?" Helen asked, puzzled.

"The faeries."

"But the fairies are already here. I saw loads of them last winter. Lavender and her aunts aren't a threat to anyone. If they hunted with horns and hounds no one would notice ..."

"Not the twinkly little flower fairies!" Sylvie said in exasperation. "The *faeries!*"

Helen looked confused.

"She can't see the different spelling when you just shout it," Yann pointed out.

Sylvie spoke quietly and slowly. "The Faery Queen and her band. The faeries of the forest, with no wings and no wands, but magic enough to be mischievous and malicious. The faeries that steal away children and leave sickly changelings in their cribs. The faeries that love human music; that enchant and beglamour fiddlers, pipers and harpists into their parties and never let them go.

"Those are the faeries that threaten my pack's land. The faeries that you, human girl, must fear."

"Don't worry about me," Helen said. "I don't sleep in a crib and I won't be enticed into any parties by a glamorous faery."

"No, of course not! You know all about fabled beasts and magical people. You are far too clever to be enticed and enchanted."

Sylvie looked casually at her long curved nails. "When are you performing?"

"Midsummer night."

"Really? Where are you performing?"

"An atmospheric venue, the Professor said … but she didn't say exactly where."

"Really? And to whom are you performing?"

Helen shifted uncomfortably on the couch. "A specially invited audience."

"Really? Do you know who they are?"

"No, I don't. Professor Greenhill said they're great patrons of music."

Sylvie laughed. "So, on the most magical night of the year, when the barriers between this world and others are thinnest, you will play your fiddle to a mystery audience, at a mystery location? You stupid child! I would leave you to suffer your fate, if it didn't affect my land and my pack."

"Don't be ridiculous!" Helen snapped. "This summer school and concert have been arranged by a well-known professor of music. We're here with our schools' permission. There were loads of official forms to fill in, to get a week off at the end of term. Our parents know exactly where we are. The best musicians in Europe will teach us over the next few days. This isn't some magical midnight conspiracy. It's a proper music school."

"Of course it is. Why would the Faery Queen be happy with anything less than the best? But we won't let her have it."

"Why not?" Helen asked.

"Because she's planning a home-coming party. Midsummer revels. She wants to persuade her people to settle on her old Scottish lands and for that she needs music. If it's a wonderful party, her people will stay. If her home-coming is a flop, the faeries will drift back to their own worlds. So with you and your fellow students playing the best music in Scotland, she will have the power to build a base here."

Helen shook her head. "We're only playing for one night, for no more than an hour. Surely you can put up with them on your land for that long?"

Sylvie stared straight into Helen's eyes. "Don't you read the old tales? Who has ever played at a faery ceilidh and returned the same night? Who has ever gone into a faery mound and come home while their family were still young ... or still alive? If you play for them, you will never come back. None of you. Once she gets skilled human musicians, why would she let you go?"

"Yann?" Helen looked up. He nodded.

Helen closed her eyes. She heard the music she'd been practising growing quiet in her mind. And fading with it, her chance to learn with the greatest violinists, as well as her chance to tell everyone she'd been the youngest student at Professor Greenhill's summer school.

She opened her eyes. Yann was looking at her anxiously.

Helen whispered, "I need proof."

"What?"

"This is my music, my future, my life, Yann. I'm not leaving without proof. If you prove to me that the Faery Queen is planning to kidnap me and force me to play for her until my wee sister is a granny, then I will go home. I promise. But first, I need proof."

"Don't you trust us?"

"I trust you, Yann, but I don't trust her."

Sylvie growled. "I knew it. All your stories show that humans hate wolves and love faeries. Of course you would side with them."

Helen shook her head. "I'm not siding with anyone. Not yet. Anyway, why are you helping her, Yann? Why are you here?"

He scuffed his front left hoof on the floor. "I got into trouble at home. I was spotted by a group of scouts on a night hike. There were stories in your newspapers about a four-legged boy, so Father sent me north to get me out of the way, to punish me.

"I'm missing my own family's summer solstice celebrations, so I thought I'd visit my friend Sylvie and help her fight the threatened invasion she's been worrying about for months. I didn't know the faeries' plan involved human musicians until I got here … and I certainly didn't know you would be here!"

"But do you have proof of Sylvie's story?" Helen insisted.

"I have no proof, except that her brothers are nervier than I have ever seen them, chasing their tails every night. I have no reason to disbelieve Sylvie and we all know how unpredictable and malicious the faeries can be. So it would be much safer for us all if you left this school."

"What about the rest of the students? Even if I do believe you and go home, I can't leave them to be stolen by the Faery Queen when she hijacks the concert."

"That's why we came tonight," said Yann. "We won't let anyone be taken by the faery folk."

Then they heard a scream.

Chapter 3

The scream wasn't as loud as the crash which had got Helen out of bed, but it lasted longer; a sustained note of panic.

The three of them rushed into the corridor. Through the window above the side door leading into the car park, they could see torchlight wavering. There were already people out there.

Helen led them to the other end of the hallway, to the door leading from Murray Wing into the old lodge. As she pushed it open, she heard worried voices echoing round the big dining room. It wasn't safe to leave that way either.

They crept back to the side door. Yann leaned into the rehearsal room and clicked the light off, looking unreasonably pleased at his understanding of human technology. "If there isn't any light behind us, perhaps no one will see us leave."

Sylvie eased the door open. Yann whispered to Helen, "We'll wait at the edge of the forest. Come to the pine tree shattered by lightning, to tell us what that scream means."

As the fabled beasts stepped warily into the dark, Yann asked, "Do you want to ride or run, Sylvie?"

"Ride," Helen ordered. "If you change too soon, the bandage will come off and the wound will bleed again."

Sylvie pulled herself up onto Yann's back and he walked into the darkness on soft hooves.

Helen stood in the doorway. The screaming had stopped, but now she could hear running footsteps.

She didn't move. She hadn't come to Dorry Shee to save the world. She wasn't here to fight a battle over land or queens or magic.

She was here to play music.

She shouldn't get involved. She should go back to bed, then get up nice and early to tackle that tricky double-stopping in the first movement of Professor Greenhill's masterpiece.

Then she noticed the weight hanging from her left shoulder. If she had come here just for the music, just for herself, why had she brought her first aid kit? She had packed bandages, swabs, splints and sutures, just as carefully as her bow and rosin. Had she hoped that she might meet her fabled friends again; that they might need her first aid kit and lead her into more adventures? If Yann's fanged friend was right, she wouldn't just be helping them, she'd be saving herself too.

So, reluctantly, she left Murray Wing, and walked

past the barn, where she would soon be rehearsing, towards the gamekeeper's cottage at the far end of the car park.

Threads of torchlight were tangling around the cottage. People were yelling, "James? James!"

Helen stepped closer. Someone caught her bare toes in a beam of light and shouted, "Here!"

Suddenly Helen was blinded by brightness, just like being on stage.

"That's not James! He's only five!"

"Go back to bed, lass, we don't need more lost children!"

"Here! Here he is!"

Mrs McGregor, the lodge owner, ran round the side of the cottage, clutching a small boy. "He's cold and sleepy, but he's fine!"

Helen stood back, while the adults with torches congratulated themselves on dealing with the crisis and walked back to the lodge for a warming drink, then she watched Mrs McGregor carry the boy into the cottage.

Helen peered through the open door, straight into the cosy living room. Mrs McGregor was sitting on a couch, hugging the little person in her arms.

"Do you need anything? Blankets to warm him up?" Helen asked gently.

"No, thanks. He must have wandered off when I went across to the lodge to chat to the caterer. He'll be fine. I'll just cuddle him warm."

Then Helen saw the other child, at the other end of the couch. A younger girl, not much older than her own little sister. The girl's eyes were wide open, terrified.

"That's not James," the little girl said clearly.

"Of course this is James!" her mum answered.

"That's not James. They took James. That's just a doll."

"Shush, Emma. This is James. He'll play with you again when he wakes up at breakfast time."

"That's not James. They took James."

Her mum was about to shush her again, but Helen took a step nearer and asked, "Who took him?"

"Shiny fast people," said Emma. "They were trying to push a doll of James in the bed when they heard Mummy coming back. They jumped out the window with James and dropped the doll on the ground. That's not James, that's the doll."

"This is James," said Mrs McGregor firmly, "and he'll be fine when he's warmed up."

She smiled at Helen, who tried very hard to smile back.

Helen ran back to Murray Wing, where she could hear the murmur and laughter of half-awake teenagers in the kitchen, and rushed up to her room before anyone realized she was out of bed too.

Helen changed into her jeans and fleece – even though it was nearly midsummer, it was cold in the Highlands in the middle of the night – pulled on her boots and grabbed the rucksack again.

On her way out, she glanced at the clipboard on the small table in the corridor. The students had to write where they were beside their name, so the teachers could find them if necessary. It was very informal, but the Professor had talked about musicians in orchestras trusting each other and how she could rely on everyone to be honest and sensible.

So Helen did wonder about writing: 1:30am. Gone to forest to see fabled beasts, by her name, but thought that would be more honest than sensible. Instead she just left the words she'd written earlier: 11pm. Gone to bed, as she was sure no one would bother checking at this time of night.

Helen walked briskly round the west side of the lodge, past the dark windows of Sinclair Wing, and onto the narrow track behind the lodge.

Under the clear black sky she was comforted by the stars she knew from home: the Pole Star and the Plough twinkling ahead of her as she walked north towards Dorry Shee Forest and the Summer Triangle hanging in the sky behind her.

When she reached the edge of the forest she couldn't make out any individual trees, nor could she find a tree blackened by lightning: they were all blackened by night. What a daft suggestion of Yann's!

The track turned west along the treeline; only a narrow footpath led east. So Helen followed the track, humming the tune she had played for Yann's people last winter solstice, hoping he would hear her. After ten minutes with no sign of a lightning tree or her friend, she spun round and walked east again. She passed the point where the track turned to the lodge, and continued eastwards along the forest edge, stumbling occasionally on the rougher, narrower path.

She kept humming, though now she was adding fancy, slightly sarcastic, twiddles to the end of each verse.

Suddenly she saw Yann's tree. Not blackened by lightning as she had assumed, but ripped open to reveal its white flesh, clear and bright against the night forest. Not such a bad idea after all. Helen strode to the scarred tree.

Yann stepped out, grasped her shoulder and pulled her into the trees. He guided her twenty paces into the forest, to a clearing dominated by a huge smooth-trunked beech tree. Sylvie was crouched beside a small fire, her silver hair glowing and her golden eyes sparkling. She smiled at Helen, showing only the tips of her teeth.

"I thought wolves were afraid of fire," Helen said.

"They are, but I'm not. One advantage of being a wolf girl, rather than a true wolf!" Sylvie laughed, more relaxed in the forest than in the lodge.

Helen glanced at Sylvie's arm. The bandage was still secure.

"Tell us about the scream," ordered Yann impatiently.

Helen thought about the best way to describe the facts. "The lodge owner screamed because her five-year-old son was missing. Then she found a small boy asleep outside. The boy's wee sister said some shiny fast people had taken her brother and left the sleeping boy, which she called a doll. His mother thinks the boy is just cold and needs a cuddle."

"What do you think?" asked Yann.

Helen sighed. "I think there's a chance the faeries took James and left a changeling in his place."

"It's not a changeling," said Sylvie. "It's not one of their own to replace the boy; just an image of him, to buy them time to carry the boy off. The cold, sleepy boy will sicken over the next few days ... and be dead a day or two after midsummer."

"Dead!" Helen shivered and moved nearer the fire.

"Don't worry. What you call a doll is really a stock; a boy shape, carved from an ancient tree trunk. It's not alive. But the real boy is alive and with the faeries. I wonder why they want him?"

"I don't care why they want him," snapped Helen, shocked at Sylvie's lack of concern. "I just need to know how to get him back. He has a wee sister who wants to play with him and a mum who wants to cuddle him."

She turned to her friend. "Yann, how do we get him back?"

"Children stolen by the faeries can't come back, Helen. I'm sorry."

"Nonsense. Tam Linn came back."

"Hundreds of years later."

"Thomas the Rhymer came back."

"He was a grown man when they took him and he returned to the faeries in the end."

"There must be others who came back!"

"No point getting him back," murmured Sylvie. "He'll just crumble to dust."

"What?" Helen backed away from this girl who could tell her nothing but bad news.

"If he eats faery food, then the first time he puts human food in his mouth, he'll crumble to dust. Whether you get him out in five minutes or fifty years, if he has eaten faery food, you can never save him." She smiled up at Helen. "But you believe me about the faeries now, don't you?"

"Yes. *No!* This isn't proof. This is just guesswork from a wee girl's nightmare. But *if* they have the boy and *if* he hasn't eaten faery food and *if* we can find him in time … HOW DO WE GET HIM BACK?"

A new voice answered her. "You feed him human food, so he doesn't hunger for faery food. Then you give the Faery Queen exactly what she wants in return for his freedom."

Helen whirled round. A boy stepped into the clearing.

He was tall and slim and shining. His pale face was smooth, with high cheeks and a straight nose. His hair was thick gold, his eyes clear blue and his teeth shone whiter than Sylvie's. When he smiled he lit the clearing more brightly than the fire.

He was dressed in green. Dark green silk, fitted and flowing, embroidered with animals and leaves which moved in the firelight even once he stood still. He wore a long sword on his left hip.

Helen couldn't stop staring at him. She needed to see him clearly. She needed to get closer.

"HELEN!" shouted Yann. "It's not real! How he looks is not real. It's glamour. He plays with light and colour and shape to enchant your eyes, the way you work with pitch and volume and rhythm to enchant my ears."

Helen took a step back and looked harder at the boy.

Sylvie stood up. She spoke, bitingly polite. "Good evening, Faery. I hope you enjoy your short stay in my forest and have happy memories of these trees when you return home. Your own home, far from here."

The beautiful boy in green bowed, replying in a light cheerful voice, "Thank you, Wolf. I hope you have enjoyed your holiday in our homeland. You will take our fondest wishes with you as your pack moves to new hunting grounds."

Sylvie smiled with all her teeth. Helen could see her measuring the distance to the boy's throat.

Yann said calmly, "Don't provoke her, Faery, or we'll all regret it. You're not welcome in this forest. Just leave now."

"I would certainly regret being somewhere I wasn't wanted. I'll go away then, shall I? I'll go away and leave you to ponder your ignorance about faery diplomacy. I'll go away and leave you to wonder how to return that defenceless child to his mother's arms. Farewell. Good luck with the impossible." He turned and walked out of the firelight.

"No!" yelled Helen desperately. "Please come back! Please stay!" Then she remembered why she wanted him to come back. "Please tell us how to save the boy."

The faery turned and smiled at her. Helen felt herself drawn towards the glow of his skin, the shine of his clothes and the perfection of his smile. She twisted music from wood, metal and air. What was he twisting light and beauty from? She half-closed her eyes, looked carefully past the shimmer and, just for a moment, glimpsed a painful red spot by his left nostril.

She grinned. "I'm Helen Strang and I'll be very grateful for any information you can give us."

He laughed. "I'm Lee Vale and I'll do my best to help you."

Yann and Sylvie spoke together. "Why would you help us?" "Don't trust him!"

Then Yann said loudly, "I don't believe you are called Lee. That's not a faery name. I certainly won't trust you if you won't give us your true name."

The boy blushed under his shine. "Lee *is* my name."

"It can't be. Faeries must be named for a plant that has its roots in the earth. What is your *true* name?"

"It's kind of my name." He kicked the toes of his long red boots in the leaf litter.

"It can't be," Yann insisted.

"It's *short* for my name."

"What's your full name then?"

"If I tell you, will you still call me Lee?"

Yann snorted but Helen said, "Yes, I'll call you what you like."

"My name is …" his voice dropped so low Helen almost couldn't hear it over the crackling flames. "Oh, I shouldn't have to do this …"

Yann pointed at the faery. "Let me guess! Lee is short for … Lily! Lileee! Your name is Lily! Isn't it?"

The boy lifted his chin and glared at the centaur laughing above him. "Yes! The lily is a plant to be proud of; not just a beautiful flower, but a powerful poison too."

"But it's like being called Daisy or Rosie or Poppy! Don't most male faeries get tree names, like Oak or Rowan or Larch? But you got Lily! What kind of lily are you, anyway? A wet water lily?"

"A tiger lily?" growled Sylvie.

"A tiny little lily of the valley?" Yann suggested. Lee scowled. Helen remembered his last name was Vale.

"There's nothing wrong with the name Lily!" she broke in. "I have a cousin called Lily." She needed the faery boy, whatever he was called, to stay and help them, not be driven off by Yann's taunts.

But Yann wouldn't leave it alone. "Is your cousin a boy, or is your cousin a *girl?*"

She shrugged. "A girl."

"A girl. It's a girl's name. Hi, Lily. Love the green blouse."

"It may be a girl's name for humans," Helen turned to the faery, "but I'm sure it's a perfectly good boy's name among the faeries."

He smiled gratefully. "I was named after my grandfather, but he was named after his great-aunt, so I prefer Lee."

"Well, Lee, can you tell us how to rescue the boy?"

"I don't care what you're called," snarled Sylvie. "I'll only be grateful when you get out of my forest."

"Put your teeth away, Sylvie," spluttered Yann, making an effort to stop laughing. "We must try to get the boy back, or when that faery stock is found in his bed, hundreds of folklore hunters will start searching your forest. Let Helen talk to this Lily."

Sylvie glowered at the faery. Yann stepped back to give Helen and the boy space. Helen said, "So, Lee, can you help us?"

"If you will give me your trust, I will give you my help." Lee smiled so brightly that Helen was nearly knocked over by the force of it. He's got a spot, she chanted to herself, *he's got a spot.*

She nodded. "I will trust you, if you will help us."

Yann groaned. Helen had made her first bargain with the faery folk.

Chapter 4

"Your wolf is right, Helen," Lee said as they all sat round the fire. "You must not let the boy eat faery food, because once he has, he can't live in your world. Guests who have tired of our hospitality have gone home, to discover their families grown old or died … and when a kind neighbour has comforted them with soup or stew, they have crumbled to dust. So if you want the boy back, you must stop him eating faery food."

"How?" Helen asked eagerly.

"Feed him human food, of course."

"If we can get food to him, can't we just grab him and get him out?"

"It's not that simple. It's easier to enter the faery world than to escape from it. I can find a window through which you can give him food, but for a doorway through which he can walk out, you'll have to bargain with the Faery Queen."

"What can we bargain with?" Helen asked, prodding the ground with a bent stick.

Lee smiled. "What do you have, Helen?"

Helen stared into the fire. "Music," she whispered. "I have music."

"No!" boomed Yann. "I won't let you give yourself away for a child you don't even know. There must be another way."

"I doubt it," said Sylvie. "That's probably why they stole the boy … to force the musicians to play. He's a hostage. Your music is the ransom."

Helen shook her head. "Nobody needs a hostage to hear our music, we're here because we *want* to play. If the students don't know the Faery Queen is planning to hijack our concert, they'll play at midsummer without needing to be forced or persuaded."

Sylvie shrugged. "She may have taken him in case someone sharper than you works it out before midsummer."

"Or perhaps she knows you played selkie music at our winter gathering," Yann said. "Perhaps she's worried you'll recognise the ways of magical beings and be a danger to her plans."

"She stole the boy so she could bargain with *me?*" Helen took a deep breath. She had to think about the boy, not herself. "If she's holding James for ransom, then we have until the end of the week to find something else to bargain with, because presumably she'll want us to play at our best, and we won't have rehearsed together often enough to play perfectly until midsummer night."

"If the boy is to have any value as a hostage," added Yann, "he must be able to return home safely, so perhaps she won't make it too difficult to feed him human food. Do you have food in your bag, healer's child?"

"No." Helen almost laughed. "It's not a picnic basket, it's a first aid kit."

"I could hunt a snack for him," offered Sylvie.

"I don't think a five-year-old boy will eat raw meat," said Yann.

"There's no rush to feed him." Lee was leaning back on his hands watching them talk. "Particularly not if you're going to work everything out so fast. You hardly need me!"

"But we have to get human food to him before he eats faery food and he's already been with them more than an hour. We have to get food to him right now!" Helen insisted.

Lee shook his head. "My people cast a spell to keep children quiet as they carry them off. He won't wake until tomorrow evening, so he won't need food until then."

"Once we've fed him, how do we bargain for his release?" Helen twisted the branch between her fingers. "Do we need to see the Queen?"

Lee stared at her. She wondered if he could see past her questions and her concern for the child. She hoped he couldn't see the flicker of excitement she felt at the idea of performing for such a legendary music-loving audience.

"You must exchange messages with her," Lee said, "but I hope you won't have to speak to the Queen herself. It's not wise for humans to see the Faery Queen. You might forget what you really want." Lee stood up. "I'll meet you here tomorrow, three hours before sunset, and I'll show you a way to feed the boy. Bring food, Helen Strang, but don't bring your grumpy friends. We'll manage better with four quiet feet, rather than a whole farmyard of hooves and paws."

"I'll meet you here, but so will Yann and Sylvie, if they want. We work together."

"Your trust is touching. Just don't turn your back on the wolf … she looks hungry." Lee bowed to them all in turn. "The prospect of seeing you tomorrow is all that will brighten the bleak day I must spend without you!"

He spoiled the effect of the flowery speech with a cheery wave, stepped into the trees and was gone.

Helen threw the broken stick on the fire and watched the bark blaze.

"We can't trust him," muttered Sylvie. "He lies about what he looks like. He lies about his name. He's bound to be lying about everything else. Faeries always do."

"He probably is working for the Faery Queen," agreed Yann. "The faeries probably sent him to tell you that the boy is forfeit unless you play at their revels. So he isn't on our side, he's on hers. We can't trust him."

Helen shook her head. "I'm not sure. If he's just a messenger, why did he ask for our trust? We should judge him on the help he gives us, not what kind of being he is. Anyway, whatever side he's on, he's offered to help us feed James and negotiate his return, so he's our best chance to free James. We have to work with him."

"No, we don't!" snapped Sylvie. "This is all upside down! Yann, we came out tonight to drive these humans away. Instead we're now helping this human bargain with the Faery Queen! They should abandon the lost child, go away and let her party fizzle out."

"We can't leave the child with the faeries, not if there's a way to get him back," Yann said gently. "It's not wise, because it would draw attention to all the forest folk. It's not right, either. You don't abandon children, even if they aren't your own kind. We can save the boy and still have time to stop the revels."

"I hope we do have time, clatter-foot. Otherwise, I will let my brothers loose. We'll see if the musicians at the lodge want to play their party tunes with a pack of wolves at their backs."

Helen was about to tell Sylvie that she would never let a threat stop her playing music, when she heard a noise break the silence of the forest.

A howl.

Then a confusion of whines and barks.

"Dogs?" wondered Helen.

"Hounds!" cried Sylvie, leaping to her feet and starting to flicker.

"Don't change!" yelled Helen. "Remember the bandage!"

Sylvie solidified as a girl, but a worried-looking one.

"Hounds?" Yann looked round. "In the middle of the night?"

"I think I know whose hounds they are," Sylvie gasped.

The wolf girl sprang onto Yann's back, then leapt to

the lowest branch of the beech tree. Helen followed, ignoring Yann's complaints. "Thanks, girls. Just use me as a stepping stone. Just leave me down here."

"We're not staying up here," Sylvie called down. "I just need to see if I'm right about those hounds."

Helen clambered up the tree after Sylvie, finding and testing branches by feel once she was above the glow of the firelight. When they reached the top of the massive beech tree, they looked over the forest, its dark waves tipped with starlight.

Sylvie pointed west, to a dark lump in the middle of a treeless space. "That's the bright green mound, the ceremonial entrance to the faeries' world."

Suddenly, Helen saw the mound clearly, as the starlight was brightened by torches, held by shadowy figures, flames sputtering orange above a pack of pale hounds, tiny in the distance.

"What are they doing?" whispered Helen.

Sylvie looked up into the star-speckled sky, glancing north then south. "There's Ursus, the bear constellation … and there's Altair, the flying eagle, at the base of the triangle. Both predators visible tonight; both looking hungry in the sky. It's a night for hunters.

"So this must be the faeries' wild ride. Their Wild Hunt. They're celebrating their brave capture of a sleeping child, or marking the start of their midsummer revels. We must warn Yann."

"Don't worry about him. Yann can run faster than a hound."

"That's what I'm afraid of!" Sylvie clambered down, much more quickly than was safe, leaping past the last few branches to land at Yann's hooves.

Helen tumbled after Sylvie to hear her saying breathlessly "… the Wild Hunt, to mark the start of their revels!"

Yann shrugged. "No problem. Even with two of you on my back, I can outpace a pack of hounds."

"Don't try to race them!" cried Sylvie. "Haven't you heard of the Wild Hunt?"

"No," the centaur laughed, "but I go on some wild gallops myself!"

"Listen to me, Yann! It's not the speed that counts, it's the pursuit." Sylvie tried desperately to explain. "This magical hunt never stops. These hounds pursue you forever. Once you start to run, you become their prey and they hunt you forever. If you outpace them, they may never catch you, but they won't stop chasing you … not for the rest of your life. We can't let them start to chase us. We must hide."

They looked round. There were plenty of places for slim girls to hide, but where could a horse hide in a forest?

Yann took a deep breath. "I can't climb trees. I'll have to run for it."

"No!" Helen added her voice to Sylvie's pleas. "You can't gallop all over the countryside this week, Yann, I need you to help me escape the Faery Queen. And I know you love to stretch your legs, but running for the rest of your life sounds no fun."

Helen turned to Sylvie. "What happens if you just refuse to run? Do they tear you apart? Or do they find something else to chase?"

"I don't know."

They heard a ringing horn, answered by a whole pack of baying hounds.

Helen announced, "I'm not leaving Yann to find out on his own! Sylvie, please bank down the fire, then climb back up your tree. Yann, put on my fleece." She unzipped her fleece, shivering as the night air hit her t-shirt underneath. "Here, Yann. Now lie down."

He pulled the fleece on. "Lie down?"

"Yes, we'll just be a couple of sleeping children camping in the forest. And *we aren't going to run!* No matter what they do."

"But…" Yann struggled with the zip of the fleece, "but, Helen … if the faeries see a centaur, even a sleepy one, they'll know fabled beasts are in the forest with humans, and they might realize we're working together to frustrate their plans."

The wild music of the horns and hounds was getting louder. "Don't argue," she ordered. "Lie down!"

She was searching the rucksack for two small packets she'd kept after a charity race: foil blankets designed to keep body temperature up after a sweaty race, but also useful for preventing shock after injuries. She ripped the pouches open and covered Yann's horse body with the silver blankets, leaving only his fleece-covered torso and head showing. Then she lay down against his back.

Sylvie was still putting handfuls of earth on the fire.

"Hurry, Sylvie!" said Helen. "Hide up the tree!"

Sylvie looked at her with bright yellow eyes. "No, human girl. I will not be driven off my land by faery hounds. And I won't abandon Yann. Or you."

She lay down on the other side of Yann.

In the dark, with the fire almost dead, with no tail or hooves showing, they looked like a heap of human children huddled together for warmth.

So they lay there, as the hounds' wild cries got louder. Helen's legs twitched with the desire to leap up and run back to the lodge, to the safety of her duvet. She dug her fingers into the earth to hold herself there.

"Pretend to be asleep," she whispered. "And whatever they do, don't run." Helen closed her eyes.

She was "woken" by a cold nose at her throat.

She mumbled, "Wha' timezit?" and sat up, looking in dreamy surprise at the dozens of dogs around her. White dogs with russet ears and glowing green eyes. They growled at her.

"Hello dogs," she murmured, patting the nearest one on the nose.

"Do not try to make friends with them, they are working dogs," said a voice from the darkness behind the torches. A woman's voice, light, musical and somehow familiar. But very, very cold.

"What are you doing in this forest, children?"

Helen heard Sylvie yawn convincingly behind her and allowed herself to yawn too. She did feel exhausted. "We've been having a midnight feast. Sorry ..." she yawned again, "... are we on your land?"

"Not yet. What did you eat for your midnight feast?"

Helen looked round. There was, of course, no sign of food.

"What did you eat?" the voice demanded again.

"Everything!" Helen giggled. "We ate everything. Not a crumb left to offer you. Sorry."

"Shouldn't you run off home now?"

Helen peered at her watch. 3:00 am. Still an hour or so to sunrise.

"No," she smiled groggily. "I'm still sleepy."

The dogs were growling and sniffing round them. One thin female gripped a corner of silver blanket between her teeth and tugged. Sylvie rolled over in her pretend sleep and pinned the blanket down with her sore arm. Helen winced.

Dark voices behind the pack muttered "just bite them where they lie" and "that'll make them run."

The largest dog thumped his front paws on Helen's thigh. She fondled his ears. He grasped her wrist in his teeth, his breath chilly on her skin, then waited for an order. Helen yawned, as if dogs bit her every morning when she woke up.

The woman laughed. "Back off, Brodum, they're not yours yet." The dog let go.

Helen yawned again and rubbed her eyes.

"Up you get!" called the woman, in a voice used to obedience. "You should get home. Your parents will be worried about you. There will be a hot breakfast waiting for you."

"Not hungry," Helen mumbled. "Still full of food … need another snooze."

She lay down, surrounded by paws, closed her eyes and muttered, "Funny dream … furry dream … ate too much cake…" She kept her breathing slow and deep, fighting the urge to whack the dogs aside and sprint away.

"Prod them awake" and "make them run" the other voices urged.

"No," sighed the woman. "Let's find other prey. These children are too full and sleepy to lead us a decent chase. If we find them on their feet another night when the stars are hunting above, then we will chase them until they fall."

Helen pretended she was asleep as the pack of hounds leapt over her and light footsteps ran past her. She pretended so well that Yann and Sylvie had to shake her awake.

"You were great!"

"No one has ever escaped the Wild Hunt like that before!"

Helen yawned for real this time. "They won't fall for it again, so we should head home, but *don't run!*"

"I believe you now," she added, as they pulled the foil blankets off Yann, "about the faeries invading your forest. It's too late, but I believe you."

"So you got your proof then," Yann said archly. "What was it? The beautiful boy Lily?"

"No," said Helen. "The dogs. Their breath was icy cold. And that woman's voice was even colder."

"Why is it too late?" demanded Sylvie, as Helen shoved the blankets untidily into a pocket of the rucksack.

"It's too late, because I promised I would leave if you gave me proof. But I can't leave now. I have to break my promise. I have to stay and get James back."

Sylvie growled. "No! You promised to go. If you stay, the Faery Queen will get her music."

Yann frowned, then agreed with Helen. "You're right. Now that she has stolen the boy, the danger is not just to you. Perhaps you should stay. So I release you from your promise to me, healer's child, because I know you won't play for the Faery Queen once we free the boy, will you?"

Helen thought of that cold voice and shook her head. But she didn't make any more promises.

Yann and Sylvie accompanied Helen to the track. The centaur and the bandaged girl kept going along the treeline, as Helen walked slowly towards the lodge. All that yawning had tired her out far more than meeting new friends and foes, and nearly being eaten by faery hounds. She fell into bed without even unlacing her boots and fell asleep dreaming of applause so loud it spanned several worlds.

Chapter 5

The sun was high in the summer sky when Helen woke. She was stiff, still had her boots on, and had pine needles poking into her scalp.

Someone along the corridor was playing incredibly fast scales on a flute; someone else was flushing the toilet. From the boys' wings she could hear Tommy, the percussionist from Glasgow, warming up thunderously. He wasn't going to make any friends here. Not at this time in the morning.

Helen wasn't sure she was going to make friends here either.

She'd been so proud of being the youngest person selected for this summer school. But now she was here, she wished the age gap wasn't so big. She was still eleven. She'd only just finished her last year at primary school. All the other students were teenagers, already at secondary school.

The only thing she had in common with them was that they were all excellent musicians, but that wasn't enough for friendship, especially when Professor Greenhill still had to choose her soloists. They were competitors, not colleagues.

Now Helen knew there were fabled beasts and magical beings in the forest, planning to drive the students away or lure them into another world, it was going to be even harder to chat to the others like this was just another music class.

Though if she was going to be stuck with them in a faery mound for centuries, perhaps she should make an effort. So she had a quick shower and walked down to breakfast all fresh and smiling.

The night before, the students had been allocated to different wings: the girls to the Murray and Sinclair wings on the west of the lodge; the boys to the Campbell and Gordon wings on the east.

The Professor, her deputy and the visiting tutors were staying in the old lodge building which had been the original "big house." The students were in four wings built last century to turn it into a hunting, shooting and fishing lodge. The McGregors were in the final stages of renovating the lodge to turn it into tourist accommodation. The four wings would be for families, so each wing had its own kitchen and bathroom.

The renovations weren't quite finished though, Helen thought, as she stepped over a dusty toolbox on the way to the kitchen.

The students had to make their own breakfast in their

own kitchens, but would have lunch and tea in the old lodge dining room. Helen could hear the four other girls in the kitchen, arguing about whether they should each make their own breakfast or whether they should take turns, a different person making breakfast for the whole wing each morning.

Helen walked into the kitchen at an unfortunate time. Zoe, one of the other violinists, was facing the door, in mid-sentence. "… Aha. The girl wonder! Our very own primary prodigy! Are you old enough to work a toaster? Does mummy let you use electrical equipment?"

Helen sighed. Since she'd arrived at Dorry Shee she'd bandaged a wolf and faced down a pack of eternal hounds. She ought to be able to handle a teenager from Edinburgh. If she didn't stand up for herself right now, she would be the "wee girl" all week. Anyway, she needed the kitchen to herself to make a picnic.

So she smiled sweetly. "Would you let me make you breakfast? That would be fun. At home, I sit in a high chair and daddy makes me toast fingers. Would you like toast fingers, Zoe?"

Zoe scowled, and Helen wondered if she had gone a bit far, but the three other musicians round the table laughed. Juliet, the flautist, thanked Helen politely when she put the toast, butter, jam and honey on the table. Alice, the cellist, patted a chair for Helen to sit beside her.

But Helen didn't sit down, she pottered around making extra slices of toast until everyone else had gone upstairs. Then, in between bites of her own breakfast, she made jam sandwiches and cheese sandwiches, took the top six chocolate biscuits out of a new packet, rinsed a couple of red apples, and filled a plastic bottle with tap water.

She heard someone's feet stomp down the stairs and hid the picnic in a bag under the sink. Now she could enjoy a day of music lessons, before taking the food to James in the evening.

The kitchen door crashed open and Zoe marched in, wearing clumpy shoes that made her a head taller than Helen. "Aha. Still licking jam off your fingers? I hope you wash your hands before you touch your violin.

"I just want to tell you it's very important to know your place in an orchestra and I am senior to you, so that violin solo is mine. Do you understand? Do you promise not to get in my way, baby girl?"

"I've decided not to make too many promises this week. But don't worry, Zoe, being a better fiddler than you is not my main priority."

"Quite right, you just concentrate on learning what you can from me. And please remember, 'fiddle' is baby language. Big people call it a violin!" She stomped back out again.

Helen grinned. Being better than Zoe wasn't her *main* priority, but it was near the top of the list. If any audience was going to hear her play this week, they would hear her play a solo.

So she mustn't be late for her first lesson with Professor Greenhill. She dashed upstairs for her fiddle, then out of the door leading from their wing into the old lodge. She found herself in the dining room and slid to a halt. Which way was the Professor's study?

She noticed that all the windows at the south end of the dining room were huge, giving an amazing view of the loch and mountains in front of the lodge. All the windows at the back of the room were small and poky.

It was like the lodge was facing the mountains, gazing at the picture postcard landscape, but ignoring the forest at its back. Helen grinned, tempted to give a panto yell of "it's behind you!" This summer's drama was happening among the dark trees, out of sight, not in the brightly-lit mountains.

She shook her head and jogged towards the door near the front windows. It led to a long corridor decorated with big maps of Scotland; a wide corridor made narrower by piles of cardboard boxes full of "What's on in the Highlands" magazines, and empty display stands for flyers.

At the end of the hallway, she arrived at a closed door with a laminated white sign:

PROFESSOR FAY GREENHILL'S STUDY
PLEASE KNOCK
(PLEASE **DON'T** KNOCK IF YOU CAN HEAR MUSIC)

The flautist from breakfast, Juliet, was sitting outside listening to the flute music floating from the room.

Helen sat opposite her. "Are you next? I thought I was in at ten."

"No, I'm waiting for my friend, Amelia. She's had the first lesson of the whole school."

"Have you been listening? Does it sound like the Professor is a hard teacher?"

Juliet shrugged. "There's been a fair bit of good music in the last ten minutes, but it started off with a lot of nervous silence."

Helen grimaced. "I'm pretty nervous too. Playing in front of the great Professor! I bet I play my wolf note about a million times in the first five minutes."

"Your wolf note? What's that? I thought violinists used horsehair, not wolf hair!"

"I don't think wolf hair would be long enough to string a bow!" Helen smiled. "But we do have wolf notes, because some violins, especially old ones like mine, have one note that makes the whole instrument reverberate strangely, kind of eerily, like a wolf howling. When you learn which string and fingering produce your wolf note, you try to avoid it. The more nervous you are, the more danger there is of you playing it.

"Almost every cello has a wolf note, even the modern ones. Don't flutes have a dodgy note?"

Juliet shrugged. "The flute doesn't ... but flute players can do. Every time I change register suddenly, one particular note cracks. It makes me really nervous when I see that note in a piece of music near a big change."

"Does that note have a name?" Helen asked.

"Nothing as fancy as a wolf note. I just call it 'that horrid note!' If your wolf note is caused by the violin, not by your playing, why don't you just get a new violin?"

Helen laid her hand protectively on her fiddle case. "When my grandfather bought me this for my tenth birthday, he told me it was made in Perthshire, two hundred years ago, by a fiddle-maker called Duncan Gow, who claimed he was a direct descendant of Ossian, the great Celtic bard. There are only a dozen of his fiddles left in the world."

Juliet laughed. "Do you believe that?"

Helen grinned. "Not really, but it's a good story … and it's a great violin. My wolf note is a high B on the G string, which isn't that common, and I'm pretty good at avoiding it by using the D string, when the melody allows. Anyway, I love my fiddle, I don't want a different one."

The music in the study stopped. The two girls fell silent. The door creaked open and a girl with a wide smile and a narrow blue flute case came out. Juliet put an arm round her friend's shoulders as they walked up the corridor.

Helen faced the open door. Her first summer school lesson. The reason she'd worked so hard.

"Come in," said a soft warm voice.

Helen had only seen Professor Greenhill twice before. Once, when she auditioned last winter, when she had been so nervous she'd hardly looked up from her music stand; and then again last night, when the Professor had balanced on a dining room table to welcome them all to the summer school and tell them a few details about the midsummer concert.

The Professor was famous for her teaching rather than her playing. She had discovered and taught some of the best violinists, flautists, pipers and drummers in the last thirty years, several of whom were attending the summer school as teachers. She was also famous for her books on musical traditions and her popular compositions for small orchestral groups.

As Helen unpacked her fiddle and tightened her bow, the Professor looked up from her notes.

"Oh! You're the girl from …" She glanced at her red

leather folder again and smiled. "Of course, you're the girl from the Borders. I remember how enchantingly you played at your audition. Why don't you warm up for me with a nice jaunty hornpipe?"

Helen sighed with relief. She could choose a tune that went nowhere near her wolf note.

Professor Greenhill was tall and wore a tight tweed skirt and jacket, with a pair of high, spiky, patent-black shoes. A narrow scarf of many swirly colours was tied neatly round her neck and a pair of silver-framed glasses perched on the middle of her nose. Everything about her was neat and polished except her long white hair, which kept falling out of its bun as she nodded enthusiastically at Helen's playing. She seemed content to listen, encourage and appreciate. She was the perfect audience and, because of that, Helen played her best.

Helen felt the tension of last night slip away. This was why she was here; to learn and to play. To be a musician was the most wonderful gift in the world. Nothing else mattered.

"Now you've warmed up, Helen," the Professor said, as she knotted her hair in a bun again, "why don't you try the midsummer solo sections?"

Helen had been rehearsing this music for weeks. Every time she had played it, her little sister Nicola had danced around the kitchen. Even though she knew this was a mini-audition, her chance to impress before Zoe and the other violinists had their lessons, she still grinned the whole time she played, as the music flowed perfectly from her bow.

The Professor nodded joyfully, shaking her hair loose again, and made gentle helpful suggestions.

When Helen had finished, the Professor smiled. "You are a very skilled player, with lots of passion too. Lovely. Now, off you go. I will hear your wonderful interpretation of my humble tune again soon."

Helen stepped slowly into the corridor. She could have played in that study for the Professor forever if there hadn't been a queue of students building up outside.

She walked dreamily out of the lodge front doors, but the cool air blowing off the loch woke her up. She stood for a moment, staring at the magnificent mountains ahead of her, watching dozens of tiny silver burns flow down their rocky sides into the loch.

Then she remembered she had a small boy to feed that night, so she hoisted the violin case onto her back, and headed for the McGregors' cottage. Helen knocked. Mrs McGregor opened the door.

"How's James?" Helen asked.

"How nice of you to ask! He's awake, but I think he's coming down with something. He's sleepy and doesn't want to eat."

Helen looked into the small living room. The little girl was at the table, rattling buttons in a bowl; the boy was sitting straight up on the couch, covered by a blanket.

Helen stared at him. He had been lying down last night, now he was sitting up! Surely a wooden statue couldn't do that! If James was at home after all, then the Faery Queen didn't have a hostage and no one would have to play at her revels.

"Hello!" Helen said.

"Hello!" the boy replied, with exactly the same intonation.

"How are you, James?"

He didn't answer, just stared ahead with half-shut eyes.

His mum said, "He got a bit of a chill last night. He'll be better soon."

"Better soon," he agreed.

Helen frowned. He was just repeating other people's words. He wasn't really talking.

Then the boy turned to Mrs McGregor, with a slight creak that might have been the couch, or might have been his stiff shoulders, and gave her a blindingly bright smile.

She laughed. "That's my boy!"

Helen shivered. She'd seen a smile that bright last night. She'd better take the picnic into the forest tonight after all.

She sighed. "Would you like me to play with Emma for a while? She's the same age as my wee sister and it would give you both some peace and quiet."

Mrs McGregor smiled. "That would be great. I'm too busy to play with her just now, with James under the weather and their dad away on an outdoor activities course in Fort William, so I'm sure Emma would love someone to play with."

Helen held her hand out to Emma. "Let's go and make a noise somewhere else, shall we?"

Emma trotted along beside her to the rehearsal room in Murray Wing. It was just as messy as Yann and Sylvie had left it after their attempted sabotage: the bookcase squint against the armchair; loose music all over the couch; the bent music stand flung in a corner; the ripped drums under the shelves.

Perhaps teenagers didn't notice mess. Or perhaps they assumed someone else would tidy it up.

Helen offered Emma an intact African drum to bang and spent five minutes clearing up to the noise of elephants crossing the savannah. Helen grinned. Her own wee sister used drums for animal noises too.

She sat down beside the three-year-old. "What does James like to eat?"

"Birthday cake," answered Emma, still tapping the drum.

"Cake?"

"Just birthday cake, but he doesn't eat the candles."

"I'm glad he doesn't eat the candles. Does he like apples?"

"No." Emma's voice was firm.

"What about chocolate biscuits?"

"No. I like chocolate biscuits." Emma smiled up at Helen.

"I'll get you one in a minute. What *does* James eat then? Does he eat sandwiches?"

"Chocolate biscuit?"

Helen wasn't going to get any more answers until she had produced a chocolate biscuit. She nipped into the kitchen and got Emma two chocolate biscuits.

When the little girl had finished getting chocolate all over herself and the genuine African djembe, Helen tried again. "Does James like cheese sandwiches?"

"No."

Helen sighed. Just her luck to have to find life-saving, non-magical food for the fussiest boy in Scotland.

"Does he like jam sandwiches?"

Emma nodded. "Yes."

Helen gave Emma a hug.

"But just jam," Emma added. "No butter. Just jam. And bread."

"Absolutely. You need the bread or it isn't a sandwich. What else does James eat?"

"Birthday cake."

Helen was right back where she'd started. "Okay. Do you like picnics, Emma?"

She brought the whole picnic bag through to the tiny three-year-old, and while Emma ate all the food her brother wouldn't touch, Helen made another batch of sandwiches with just jam, no butter. Making a wild guess about James's attitude to crusts, she cut them off too.

She filled a bag with jam sandwiches and nothing else; all that stood between James and a lifetime with the faeries. She hoped the lodge wouldn't run out of jam by the end of the week.

She wiped most of the chocolate off Emma, then took her back to the cottage. Mrs McGregor and the boy had fallen asleep beside each other. Emma was yawning, so Helen laid her down at the other end of the couch.

She took another look at the sleeping James, so she would recognise the real thing tonight.

Then she headed to the old lodge for lunch and her afternoon lessons. The first couple of hours with a composer from Dublin on orchestration, arranging and improvisation passed quickly. But the music theory lesson afterwards wasn't exciting enough to keep her mind off faeries and wolves. It was an individual lesson with Dr Lermontov, the Professor's deputy at the summer school, the only other teacher staying for the whole week. He was a world expert on the use of harmony and counterpoint.

When Helen realized that the shiny new décor in the Doctor's study included atmospheric photos of duns, brochs and faery mounds, she found herself staring at them over Dr Lermontov's round bear-like shoulders. Really, she should be researching faery weaknesses, not thinking about four-part harmony.

"Miss Strange!" Dr Lermontov shouted.

Helen jerked round. "Strang, sir, my name is Strang, not Strange."

"Miss Stran-ga, you must listen to me with your eyes as well as your ears if you are to learn from me. Stop looking at the walls; look at me and my manuscripts!"

So Helen followed his pen nib across the staves and tried to concentrate. It was a huge relief when he picked up his violin so they could play a duet. Dr Lermontov was a virtuoso violinist, but he was also a good enough teacher to let her play the challenging music and keep the supporting role for himself.

He smiled at her as they put their violins away. "At least you concentrate totally on your violin when she is in your hands. But perhaps when I want you to concentrate on soprano, alto, tenor and bass, the call of the summer sun is stronger!"

"No," answered Helen, "it's the summer night that calls me."

Dr Lermontov said, "In the north of Russia, the summer nights are so short, the sky never grows dark."

Helen smiled back at him and took a chance. "Do you know where we're playing on midsummer night, Dr Lermontov?"

"No, Miss Strange, I was summoned across the world to play in this concert, but even I do not know where it will be. Fay Greenhill says it will be a night to remember forever, so I will be content to see our stage and our audience when the sun goes down and not before."

"Is that wise?"

"Wise? Wise? Artists must take risks! Anyway, it does not matter where we play nor to whom we play. In a cowshed to farmers? Or in a palace to tsars? It does not matter … so long as we play with all our hearts! The music matters, not the venue, nor the audience."

"Nor the theory?" Helen asked quietly.

"Indeed!" He laughed a deep growly laugh. "Not the theory either, my clever strange girl. Do not worry about the concert. I trust Professor Greenhill completely. Now off you go for your tea and let the summer night come to you."

So Helen went down the wide stairs to the dining room. For a whole hour of stilted conversation over large plates of pasta, she gazed impatiently out of the window at the evening shadows moving slowly towards the eastern side of the glen.

She left before pudding, got the just-jam sandwiches and a bottle of water out of the kitchen, then put her violin case into the wardrobe and the rucksack on her back.

As she left, she scribbled: Early night on the clip-board. She didn't claim she was in bed. She was just having an early start to her night's adventures. So it wasn't really a lie.

Chapter 6

Helen reached the lightning tree slightly early for the rendezvous. She stepped into the cool shadow of the forest and found the clearing by following the faint smell of burnt bark.

She sat down, murmuring, "Who needs a wolf? There's nothing wrong with my nose!"

"There's nothing wrong with your nose at all, fair maiden," said a voice in her ear. "You have a perfect nose, an alabaster complexion, the musical fingers of Orpheus, the enticing scent of jam …"

Lee stepped flamboyantly in front of her, sweeping a wide red hat off his head, and bowed low, his knee bent and the feather on his hat brushing her toes.

"The courage of a lion too, to come here unaccompanied."

He lifted her hand and kissed the back of it.

Helen laughed out loud, a snort of surprise and embarrassment.

Lee dropped her hand, put the hat on his head and said in a less dramatic voice, "Oh dear. Too much?"

"Far too much!"

"So what level of charm and glamour would you be comfortable with?"

"Your normal self would be fine."

"I don't think I have a normal self." He flicked his red cloak out of the way and flopped down on the ground beside her.

"Are you always playing a part?" Helen asked.

"Of course. Aren't you?"

"No!" Helen answered firmly. Then she wondered. She'd played the part of a big sister this afternoon, to find out about James's eating habits. Did she ever play any other parts? Was she always the same Helen?

Lee smiled. "So, shall I just tell you how clever and talented you are, then we can move on?"

"Alright. But no hand kissing."

"None?"

"None at all."

"Excellent. Let's go and feed your stolen child." He stood up.

"Shouldn't we wait for the others?"

"Why? You don't think they care about your boy, do you? He doesn't have enough legs or hair or tails for a wolf or a centaur to bother about him. Come on."

Helen didn't stand up. "Lee … I don't think I should follow you into the forest on my own. I think it would be safer to wait for Yann and Sylvie."

"Don't you trust me?" He raised his eyebrows. "You promised to trust me!"

"I'd be very silly to trust you completely, wouldn't I?"

He looked downcast. "Usually, it would be dangerous for a human child to trust a faery." Then he grinned at her. "But this summer, in this forest, I'm entirely on your side. You *can* trust me. So let's get going."

"Why are you on our side? Aren't you one of the Faery Queen's subjects?"

"No one is her subject! We're all just guests at her endless parties. No, I am a loyal subject of ..."

As his voice trailed away, Helen noticed that his red cloak had darkened to a less flattering mud-brown. She turned to see what had surprised him.

A blue dragon was shouldering through the trees. Trunks and branches were bending away from the huge body, then springing back into place over the long spiky tail.

Helen stood up, moving quickly between the faery and the dragon. "Hello, Sapphire," she called. "Have you grown *again?*" The dragon blew a cheerful flurry of sparks at Helen, who ducked. "Wow. Your fire's hotter too!"

Lee said, very formally, "Fair maiden, are you acquainted with this dragon?"

"Of course! She's my biggest and warmest friend!"

Sapphire blew an arrow of sparks over Helen towards Lee. The feather on his hat caught fire. He whacked it on the ground to extinguish it.

"I think that was a warning," said Yann briskly, emerging from behind Sapphire. "A warning not to betray us, *Lily,* or our dragon will be annoyed."

"Your dragon," said Lee, "has struggled to get ten trees' depth into my forest and will get trapped in a maze of branches if she tries to go further. I'm not afraid of her."

Sapphire blew a real flame this time, setting a small bush on fire.

"Of course," sighed Lee. "Trees burn."

"Don't burn the forest!" called Sylvie, from the other side of the dragon. "It's not a faery forest yet."

Suddenly a tiny lilac raincloud appeared above the flames, soaking the leaves and branches so effectively that the fire was out within seconds. The raincloud then floated through the air and started to drip carelessly on Lee's hat. The charred feather drooped as he tried to look dignified with water running down his neck.

"Stop teasing him!" Helen grabbed Lee's elbow and pulled him out from under the cloud. "If you keep teasing him he might not tell us how to find James. Anyway, it's not kind or fair."

Threads of vapour drifted away from the cloud and the purple at its centre became clearer. Helen suddenly realized who it was. "Lavender! You're doing even fancier weather spells now! You aren't even wet!"

The robin-sized flower fairy, a sharp sparkle of blonde hair and purple satin, landed gracefully on Helen's hand. "Sapphire and I came as soon as Yann sent a message saying the Faery Queen wanted to steal our favourite fiddler."

"Where are Rona and Catesby?" Helen looked round for the other fabled beasts she'd quested with last winter.

"Catesby's fledgling feathers aren't strong enough

to fly this far and the last we heard of Rona, she was following some fantastic fish towards the Arctic Circle.

"But we're here. You have Sylvie's teeth, Yann's bravery, my magic and Sapphire's fire. We will protect you, Helen."

"Don't worry about me. It's James we need to protect. I'm sure your talents will be very handy, but Lee is the only one who can lead us to the boy."

They all turned to look at the faery. Dry and dapper again, he smiled at his audience. "What an unexpected pleasure to see so many of you, but you can't all follow me. The Faery Queen might let Helen feed her hostage, but it would be foolishly provocative to approach her domain with all your clattering, howling and sparking. So ..." he shrugged regretfully, grinning cheerfully at the same time, "I think I should take Helen to the boy by myself."

"No!" A variety of voices yelled in disagreement.

"If you don't want someone big or noisy to come with us," Helen said to Lee, "why doesn't Lavender come?" Helen would feel safer approaching the lands of a powerful magical being with someone she truly trusted by her side or, at least, by her ear.

Lee glanced at Lavender. "Ah yes ... the raindrop fairy. What other party tricks does she do? Sneaking under pillows for teeth? Performing in pantomimes and puppet shows?" He shrugged. "Bring her if you like, no one will notice."

"If you betray Helen to that harpie of a Queen, then you will notice me and my power, you foppish feather-thief," Lavender shouted. Lee cupped his hand round his ear, as if he couldn't quite hear her.

Lavender snorted and flew to Helen's right shoulder.

"I don't clatter or spark. I shall come too," announced Sylvie.

"No," said Lee. "Three is enough."

"This is my forest and if you don't take me, I will follow you. You would far rather have me walk where you can see me, faery, than have me creep up behind you."

Lee sighed extravagantly. "Very well. Four of us. But we stay hidden when we get there. No one looking out of the window from the faery world must see anyone but Helen. They must not even see me!"

"Why not you?" Yann demanded. "What are you afraid of, Lily-livered boy? Afraid the Queen might criticize that combination of green waistcoat and red hat?"

"No," snapped Lee. "I'm afraid that if the Queen hears I've been seen with a human child and a wolf, then she might grab Helen right now, to stop the human girl creating a wider alliance among her enemies."

He turned to Helen. "I will show you the path to the boy and the path back, but when you're feeding the boy, you must stand alone. Will you trust me?"

Helen glanced round at her friends. Sylvie was scratching her grubby bandage and wouldn't meet Helen's eyes. Lavender was fluttering with indecision. Sapphire shrugged her massive blue shoulders. Yann gave a tight smile, "It's up to you whom you trust, Helen."

She was aware of the daylight fading into a summer evening and, keen to get the food she'd made that morning to James as soon as possible, she said, "Right.

Those of us who're going … let's go." She waved a nervous goodbye to the dragon and the centaur, as Lee led them past the beech tree, deeper into the forest.

Moving through the dark trees was more of a struggle than a stroll. There were no paths, the ground was broken up by rocks and roots, and the forest was growing on slopes as steep as the mountains on the other side of the glen.

The thick summer leaves blocked the evening light, but it was never completely dark under the trees; there was always a rocky outcrop, stretch of water or fallen tree letting patches of brightness through.

From the lodge, Dorry Shee looked like a simple pine forest, but Helen was pushing past birches, oaks and rowans, and crushing purple foxgloves, pink roses and yellow buttercups.

The forest was beautiful, but the walk was no fun at all. To keep up with Lee, Helen was forcing her way under low branches and past thorny bushes, with the constant chatter of Lavender in her ear, updating Helen on the latest magic she'd learnt, fabulous dresses she'd tried, new songs their friend Rona had written. But the fairy kept losing her way in the middle of sentences and repeating herself.

Then Helen remembered. "Lavender, are you afraid of Lee? Is that why you're nervous? You did once say to me forest faeries could eat flower fairies in one mouthful. Were you serious? Do you really think he would eat you?"

"Probably not," admitted Lavender. "Not unless someone dared him to."

"But are you afraid of him?"

"Of course, but he's afraid of me too. The faery folk have been showing off for so long that everyone knows their powers and their limitations. If you put together all the faery stories, you can get the measure of their magic. They're lazy too, so they're still relying on the magic created by their ancestors."

They emerged from a thorny thicket into a flat stretch of tall pines. Everyone moved much faster.

Lavender kept chattering. "We flower fairies keep most of our magic hidden and we're always learning new magic. So I know *how* he is dangerous and that's why I'm afraid of him; but he has no idea what I can do and that's why he's afraid of me."

"Is he afraid?" Helen looked at the confident figure swinging his cloak as he strode through the trees. Apart from the moment when he saw the dragon, Lee seemed to be enjoying himself immensely. "He doesn't look afraid."

"He's terrified," said Lavender. "Can't you tell? That's why his clothes keep fading. But he's not just scared of us. He's afraid of something else too. He would much rather not be here at all. Faeries rarely bother to do something they don't want to do. I wonder what's keeping him here?"

"Let's not ask him now. If we ask him awkward questions, he might abandon us in the forest with no idea how to get home."

The light was fading above them; the shadows around the trees were getting blacker. Helen was trying to follow Lee's colourful cloak, while watching her own footing on the uneven ground.

Then she stepped out into a blaze of light. She could

see the whole of the deep blue sky above her. She smiled at the sudden bright space and air. Then Lee gestured for her to go into the clearing without him.

They were near the window to the faeries' world and Helen had to go on alone.

She stared at the clearing ahead of her. She didn't glance back; she didn't see the low grey blur of a wolf pack slipping through the trees behind them.

Chapter 7

Huge dark shapes towered over Helen's head as she stood at the edge of the clearing.

At first Helen saw a dozen open trapdoors; all facing her, all inviting her in.

Then her focus shifted and she realized that the shapes weren't doors, but massive clumps of soil and stone, bound together by roots.

She stepped to her right, to see the clearing from a different angle. The lumps of earth were the bases of a dozen dead trees, which she could now see lying stretched across the clearing.

These tall trees had been torn from the earth, by a strong wind or a giant game of skittles.

The trees hadn't died easily. Each tree had ripped up all the earth its roots could grasp, leaving a deep hole in the ground, sheltered by a wall of soil and roots above.

The ground beneath such big trees would have been almost bare last summer, but now it was ablaze with fast-growing ferns and brambles.

But where was James? Was one of these holes his prison? Were these root caves doors to the faery world, to other worlds as well?

Helen glanced at Lee and at Sylvie, and whispered, "Is James here?"

Lee shrugged, his mud-brown cloak flying open to show his snot-green shirt. He *is* nervous, thought Helen.

Lee spoke quietly. "If you want to find him, you should try walking round sunwise."

"Sunwise?" Helen frowned.

"Clockwise," explained Lavender in her ear. "The way the sun moves across the sky. Faeries are *so* old-fashioned."

Helen hesitated. Sylvie said, "I will go with you if you want, fiddler girl."

"No! You keep Lee company here, keep an eye on … each other. I'll walk round the edge."

She looked back at Lee. "Sunwise?"

He nodded. "Be very polite and don't say anything you don't mean."

"Be polite to James?"

"No. To those who guard him."

Helen's fingers tightened on the rucksack strap.

Lee frowned. "You didn't think he would be alone?"

Helen didn't answer. Of course she had thought he would be alone!

One wee boy and a packet of sandwiches. That hadn't been too worrying.

But one wee boy guarded by human-sized faeries, while she had nothing to defend herself with but jammy pieces …

Perhaps she should have brought Yann or Sapphire rather than Lavender.

However, she had to feed James, so she imagined a clock face arranged round the clearing. If she was standing at six o'clock, to go clockwise to seven o'clock, she had to turn … left. Lavender, perching on her shoulder, murmured, "Well done."

Helen walked round the clearing sunwise. At first it was easy. The new growth was higher than her waist, but it was also springy, easy to push aside. Even the brambles were armed with soft new thorns, rather than bone-hard old weapons. As she walked, she looked into the holes. They were deep and dark, denied evening sun by the high walls of roots and stones above, but even in the shadows, Helen could see they were empty.

The circuit became more difficult when she reached the side of the clearing where the trees had crashed down. Intact branches stuck up from the slain trunks like tall fences, while broken branches and smaller trees crushed under the trunks created an unstable decking of viciously sharp wood.

Approaching the first fallen tree, Helen told Lavender to get inside her fleece so she wouldn't get scratched or stabbed. She clambered over the debris, then forced her way over the trunk.

She had to balance across splintered wood from trunk to trunk, until she had struggled over half a dozen trees. Finally, safely back in the new green growth again, she realized she'd forgotten to look for James. She stared behind her at the dead trees in their creaking graveyard. If he was there, she would send Sylvie to sniff him out.

Helen walked further round the clearing, glancing into more black entrances. No one. Nothing. No one. Nothing.

She sighed. There was only one root cave left on her sunwise circle. He probably wouldn't be there. She glanced briefly into the last hole.

James yawned at her.

He was sitting against the root wall, dim, shadowy and very far away. He had the same brown hair and freckles as the boy in the cottage, but a sleepy smile and worried eyes.

"Hello," Helen said gently. "Are you James?"

He nodded.

"I'm Helen. I know your mum and Emma, and I know you like jam sandwiches with no butter. Would you like some?"

He nodded again.

She slipped the rucksack off one shoulder, unzipping the side pocket as it swung round. She held the bag of jam sandwiches out to him.

He didn't move towards her, so she walked towards him. But her feet were terribly heavy and once she'd set them down, she couldn't lift them again.

James said something she couldn't hear.

She said to Lavender, as if the words were too big to get her mouth round, "How do I get this to him?" She felt a tickle by her ear, but she couldn't hear anything.

Not Lavender. Not the sounds of the forest. Not her own breathing.

Nor could she move her feet. Actually she could. She could move them backwards, away from the boy. She took a short step back and heard the whisper of leaves behind her. Another step backwards and she heard Lavender say, "Don't go any nearer!"

But she had to. She had to get closer to James. Dreading the heaviness and silence, Helen went forward again, hearing Lavender's voice fade, sliding her feet as close as she could to James before bumping up against a piece of clearing that just wouldn't give. Was this window to the faery world see-through but unbreakable?

The boy's mouth was still moving, but she couldn't hear him. Was he there at all? She couldn't reach him. How was she supposed to feed him?

She wanted to trust Lee and he had said this was a window through which she could feed James. So she lifted the packet of sandwiches through the thick air. It weighed as much as the rucksack but she threw it into the root cave.

The picnic didn't travel in a smooth arc, but jerked through the air as if it were bumping through a series of invisible barriers before it reached James. But finally he caught it.

Then she threw the brick-heavy bottle of water. James didn't let go of the sandwiches in time to catch it, so the water landed in the dark earth in front of him. He smiled and Helen saw his lips say "thank you."

She croaked, "Enjoy your picnic. Don't eat anything else until I come back tomorrow."

She turned to leave. It should have been easier to walk in the other direction. The air wasn't so thick. Her feet were lighter.

But walking away was made more difficult by the spears. The half circle of a dozen spear points aimed at her chest.

Noise crashed in around her. Lavender's hiccupping panic. The creaking of branches round the clearing. Her own breathing, fast and hard.

And laughter behind her. Not a child's laughter.

Helen didn't look round to see who was laughing; she recognised the voice that had controlled the hounds last night.

She looked at the troop of faeries behind the spearheads. Male and female, in flowing clothes like Lee's, though not as richly decorated, with faces as hard and threatening as the spears.

Helen glanced to where Lee and Sylvie had been standing. They were gone; vanished into the safety of the trees.

She fought her own panic. Yann would never have left her. Why had she trusted these new friends? Lavender was still here, but she was the same size as the spear points. What could she do to help?

Helen whispered, "Lavender, please do that flower fairy magic the faeries are afraid of."

"Em ... I'm starting advanced magic next term. I've been studying weather this year. I could rain on them. Or try to blow the spears aside with a strong wind. I've been learning plant lore too. I could grow really nasty herbs under their feet."

"How long would that take?"

"A season or two. That's not fast enough, is it?"

"No." Helen looked round the half circle of faeries. There didn't seem to be one more elaborately dressed, or more violently inclined, than the rest; there was no obvious leader.

The laughter behind her was still tinkling and ringing.

Helen met the eyes of the tallest faery warrior. "I'm turning round," she said clearly. The warrior nodded.

Helen turned. James was gone. So were the sandwiches. But the water bottle was still stuck in the earth.

In his place was a laughing woman.

No. Not exactly in his place. She seemed brighter than James had been, more clearly lit, but further away, as if the hole in the ground was deeper now.

Helen was beginning to doubt whether anything she saw in this earthy root cave was there at all.

Wherever the woman was, she was laughing at Helen.

So Helen stared at her. Rucksack on her shoulder, arms folded, she just stared. She wasn't being very polite, she knew that. But laughing at someone surrounded by spears wasn't polite either.

The woman's beautiful face and elegant hands stayed pale and constant in front of Helen, while the patterns and colours on her dress kept changing, sliding and slipping into each other, like an oily rainbow film on a puddle stirred by a passing car.

Though Helen knew the woman was laughing at her, she was drawn to her glowing face and hypnotic clothes. She shook her head, saying to herself, I bet she has more wrinkles than Lee has spots.

She could still hear Lavender, from the depths of her collar, running through an optimistic list of scary plants and dangerous weather. She lifted her right foot, taking a tiny step towards the toppled tree. Whatever magic had stopped her reaching the boy, it wasn't stopping her reaching the woman. The window had become a door. Helen could just jump right into the hollow.

She knew that would be a very bad idea. So she just kept staring.

Now Lavender was whispering insistently, "It's the Faery Queen."

"I'd guessed that," Helen murmured back.

"Bow to her or something."

"Why?"

"You have to show respect."

"Why? She's not showing me any."

The woman's laughter was fading.

"Jam sandwiches?" she chuckled. "Do you think a packet of sticky sandwiches will tempt him more than our faery feasts?"

Helen suspected she knew more about what James ate than this woman did, but she didn't say so. Even if she wasn't going to be polite, the best way to follow the rest of Lee's advice, to say only what she meant, was to say very little.

"So, human child, do you want the boy back?" asked the Faery Queen.

Helen nodded.

"What can you offer me in exchange that is worth more than a precious child?"

Helen wondered how to answer that. "Tell me what you value and I'll see if I can offer it."

"I want *you*."

Helen had expected that and kept her voice steady. "Just me?"

"You ... and all your friends at the music school. I want you to play your wonderful music at my midsummer revels."

The Queen smiled and spoke in a softer voice. "I know you're a great fiddler, Helen Strang. I can't wait to dance to the magical music you make."

Helen grinned. The Queen had heard of her! The Queen knew she was a great fiddler! Wouldn't it be wonderful to watch a dress like that move in time to her music? Wouldn't it be wonderful to hear a voice like that compliment her playing?

Helen hummed the first movement of Professor Greenhill's music. Lavender said something, but Helen just hummed louder. The Queen's feet tapped, the hem of her dress swayed.

Then Helen saw the bottle of water, near and not near the toes of the Queen's perfectly polished silver pumps.

She felt the weight of the rucksack on her back and remembered why she was here. She stopped humming and licked a bit of jam off her thumb.

She heard Lavender say, "Watch out for her glamour! It's in her voice, as well as her face!"

Helen thought about wrinkles. Wrinkles and spots. Then she answered the Queen. "I can't offer to bring all the summer school students."

"Why not?"

"Because I'm the youngest student there. Professor Greenhill is in charge. She decides where we play and what we play."

The Queen smiled sympathetically. "You could tell them a child's freedom depends on doing what you say."

"Do you want everyone to know that you have taken a boy? People would cut down these forests to find a missing child. They might not get him back, but they would ruin your revels and your hunting ground."

The Queen frowned and, for just a moment, Helen saw tiny wrinkles on her forehead.

"So ask me for something I *can* bring you," suggested Helen, "and give me the boy in return, then no one else will know you're here."

"I want you to play for me."

Lavender cried, "No!" She was almost spinning on Helen's shoulder, her tiny stilettos digging into Helen's collar bone.

Helen shook her head. "I can't promise that."

"I don't want anything else. I only want music. Music and dancing are the most valuable currency in our world."

"There must be something else you want."

The Queen considered for a moment. "There is one object I desire. If you can bring it to me tomorrow night, I will give you the boy. If you cannot bring it to me, you must promise to play at my midsummer revels."

"Tell me what the object is."

"No. You must promise first to give me music if you fail, before I tell you what precious object I will accept instead.

"If you do not promise me now, you will never see the boy again. I will make him jam sandwiches with my own fair hands, so if his family ever see him again he will be a boy-shaped pile of dust."

She smiled again, but her face didn't glow, it glittered like ice; she laughed again, but her laughter didn't tinkle, it cracked and boomed.

Lavender bounced beside Helen's ear. "Don't promise her anything!"

Helen couldn't see what else she could do, so she considered her words very carefully. "I promise I will provide music for your midsummer revels, if I can't bring the object you want in return for the boy. I promise."

She had just made a bargain with the Faery Queen. Lavender gasped. The Queen laughed.

Helen sighed. "What do you want?"

The Queen told her.

Chapter 8

"The Fairy Flag?" Helen said in surprise.

The Queen nodded. "The Fairy Flag, which one of my sisters gave away to a MacLeod clan chief when she fell in love with him." Helen and the Queen both gave identical snorts. "The Fairy Flag, which the MacLeods have hidden in Dunvegan Castle ever since, though they have no right to it, nor any knowledge of its real power. It's hidden from the faeries who made it, who are its true owners; it's hidden behind cut stones and filthy iron.

"Faeries can't get past iron as it weakens our magic and saps our strength, but a human girl could get past their barriers and rescue the flag. Then my people would return to this forest to touch the flag, to feel its power, to congratulate me for recapturing it." She stroked her smooth golden hair. "Yes. A powerful treasure regained is almost as good as a dance."

"What power does it have?" asked Helen.

"There is more power in one thread of that ancient banner than in all ten of your fiddling fingers, human child, and that's all you need to know. Go to Skye, bring it back for me and you will get the boy. Fail … and you will give me music instead."

Helen thought for a moment, but she couldn't see an alternative, so she nodded. "I'll bring you your flag if you'll give me James back, healthy, happy and not about to crumble to dust."

The Queen smiled. "A bargain." She picked the water bottle up. "I will take this to him as a sign of good faith."

She raised her voice. "Let her past."

Helen turned round. The spear-carriers had vanished.

She looked back to the root cave. The Queen had vanished too. Helen was alone, apart from the fairy on her shoulder.

Lavender said sharply, "That was extremely foolish, Helen. A bargain with a faery never turns out well."

Helen walked towards the edge of the clearing. Lavender kept scolding her. "Why bother taking me if you were going to ignore my advice?"

"Sorry. There wasn't any other way to save the boy."

"There's no point saving one human child, at the cost of another. And you're *my friend!* I don't want to lose you to her. Why didn't you listen to me?"

"I couldn't hear you half the time, and the rest of the time, I was actually making my own decisions."

"She enchanted you." The fairy flew around Helen's head, throwing out angry fizzing light balls.

"No, she didn't!"

"Yes, she did! You may try to bargain and play hard to get, but really you dream of performing for her, because she has enchanted you."

"That's not true!" Helen said indignantly. "She didn't enchant me! I didn't agree to perform for her! All I want is to get James back. And all we have to do is get this flag, which isn't even stealing because it's the faeries' flag anyway, then James will be safe and she won't even expect any music. It's all under control, Lavender."

Lavender harrumphed.

They had reached the trees where they'd left Lee and Sylvie, but there was no sign of the faery or the wolf girl.

"Fat lot of good they were," muttered Helen. "At least you stayed with me."

"Not that you listened to a word I said!"

"Where have they gone?"

Lavender shrugged. "Maybe they ran off at the first sign of danger."

"Wouldn't Sylvie be more likely to leap at the Faery Queen's throat than run away?"

"Whether they leapt or ran, they aren't here now. I hope you remember the path home, because I didn't see anything but your ear and your hair on the way here."

"I thought Lee would take us home, so I wasn't trying to memorize it. Can't you find our way back using a finding spell or something?"

"I can't find a forest path, Helen, it doesn't belong to anyone."

"Search for a dragon then, or a centaur."

"They don't belong to anyone either."

"Yes they do, they're our friends."

Lavender looked sceptical. "Alright. Ask me to find something of yours."

Helen smiled and said in a formal voice, "Dearest Lavender, wisest fairy, please find me my friend Sapphire." Then she whispered, "She's bright blue and bigger than Yann. She should be easier to find."

Lavender frowned. "This is serious." But she started to rotate in the air, her eyes closed and her wand searching.

In the intense stillness surrounding the fairy's effort, Helen heard a snarl.

She turned away from the spinning fairy and crept into the forest. Hoping she hadn't heard another spear-carrying faery, she pressed close to the trunk of a rough-barked tree and slid round it slowly.

As soon as she saw what lay behind the tree, she ran forward, yelling, *"Stop!"*

Helen couldn't tell who was attacking and who was defending. Lee's sword was aimed at the wolf's throat. Sylvie was crouched to spring at the faery's face.

They didn't take their eyes off each other, even when Helen shouted again.

So she stepped between them, forcing Lee to move his sword to one side. She shoved him in the chest and he fell off-balance away from the wolf. The wolf tensed to leap at him but Helen took another half step and stayed between them. Sylvie snarled and sank to the ground.

Just as Helen was recovering from the fright she had given herself, stepping so recklessly into someone else's fight, Lavender flew out of the trees. "I found Sapphire but lost you! How dare you leave me alone in the middle of a spell?"

"I had to stop them ripping each other apart, Lavender!"

Sylvie, flickering between wolf and girl, spoke in bursts of snarls and words. "Let me rip … hrrrr … coward … hrrrr … stop *me?* … ooooowwww … protect you, girl … hrrrrr… skulking hiding traitor …"

"I had to hide in the trees to keep our teamwork secret from the Queen, Sylvie." Lee slid his sword back in its scabbard. "I had to keep you hidden too, even if it was at sword-point. Helen didn't need protection, did she? She fed the boy, she got back safely. Mission accomplished." He smiled around at everyone, trying to spread calm and happiness.

Lavender said sourly, *"That* mission is accomplished. The next one might be trickier."

Lee looked at Helen. "What next mission?"

"I … em … I agreed to get the Fairy Flag from Dunvegan Castle by tomorrow night in exchange for James."

"And …?" prompted Lavender.

"And … em … and if I don't succeed, then I promised to provide music for the Queen's midsummer revels."

Sylvie and Lee looked at each other, united for the first time in horror at what Helen had done.

Helen leapt to her own defence, because it didn't look like anyone else would. "What else could I have done? I had to save James! She would have fed him faery food, if I hadn't agreed."

Lee allowed exasperation to show past his usual charm. "I warned you *not to say anything you didn't mean!"*

"I didn't say anything I didn't mean! I do mean to get the flag … and I do mean to save the boy."

Sylvie looked at her through narrowed eyes. "You are either enchanted by her, or too full of your own abilities. You have done a very stupid thing, human child."

Helen barely noticed the trees and flowers as Lee led them back. Was her bargain with the Queen really that stupid? It hadn't felt stupid. It had felt brave and clever. But no one had congratulated her on her courage and quick thinking.

When they stumbled into the beech tree clearing, Yann and Sapphire were playing 'dagger paper stone' by the campfire.

Yann leapt cheerfully to his hooves. "That didn't take too long! Will we have to do the same tomorrow night?"

"Not quite," said Helen.

He raised his eyebrows.

"Tomorrow night we need to bring her the Fairy Flag."

"The Fairy Flag?"

"Uh-huh."

"From Dunvegan Castle?"

"Mm-hmm."

Yann's voice was deep and cavernous. "Why did you agree to that?"

"Because it was the only way to save James!"

"And if you fail to bring her the flag? What's the forfeit? With the faeries, there's always a forfeit."

"If I fail, I have to provide music at midsummer."

Yann swung away from her, his hooves drumming on the dry ground.

"We can do it, Yann! Dunvegan is a tourist attraction,

not a bank vault. The flag is a bit of fabric, not the crown jewels. Lavender and Lee can do magic, you and Sapphire are fast and strong, and Sylvie … well, Sylvie's pretty scary. How hard can it be to get the Fairy Flag?"

Yann spun round to face her. "If it was easy to steal the Fairy Flag, human child, then the MacLeods wouldn't have kept it for hundreds of years."

"Well, I'm sorry!" Helen yelled back. "As the alternative was a little boy never seeing his family again, I thought I did the right thing."

"The right thing for whom, girl?" demanded Sylvie. "For your people, for this forest, or for your own ambition?"

Yann turned on Lee. "You understand the dangers of faery bargains. If you *are* on our side, why did you let her agree?"

"He ran away," said Sylvie. "As soon as the faeries appeared, he was off like a rabbit down a hole."

"And did you change and chase him, because you can't resist running prey, wolf girl?" Yann asked. "Or did you stay and help Helen?"

"Once I'd caught up with him, I did try to go back to drag her away, but this coward drew a sword on me. He said he would skin me before he let the Queen see one hair of my hide."

Yann glanced at Lee with a flash of respect, then whirled round and looked at Lavender. "Did you hide from the Faery Queen too? Or did you stay with Helen? Why didn't you warn her of the foolishness of this bargain?"

"I tried to stop her, but she wouldn't listen to me."

Helen snapped, "Why would I listen to you when your best plan was blowing their hair into their eyes!"

"Helen, that's not fair …"

Yann reared up, screaming his impatience. "I knew I should have come! I knew none of you could handle this on your own!"

Lavender was floating a wing beat from Helen's face, trying not to cry. Helen was ignoring the fairy and glowering at Yann, who was scraping angrily at the ground, flicking dry leaves up at Sylvie's scowling face.

They all took a breath and started blaming someone else again.

"She never …"

"He always …"

"You must …"

ROAR! A blaze of cold silver flame engulfed them all, then burnt off instantly, leaving them unharmed, but shocked into silence.

They turned, breathless, to look at Sapphire.

The huge blue dragon started to grunt and wheeze. Helen couldn't understand the words, but she felt the dragon's anger shake the ground.

After her first outburst, Yann, Sylvie and Lavender all stared at Lee. The faery was leaning against the beech tree, polishing his sword, an amused expression on his face.

Once Sapphire finished speaking, Yann translated for Helen. "Our wise friend asks why only the faery is not blaming everyone else for his faults. She asks why we're all arguing when we're here to help and protect each other." Yann frowned. "She asks whether we're all too small and weak to withstand enchantment."

"I'm not enchanted," everyone answered, indignantly.

Sapphire laughed. Then she spoke again. This time

Lavender flew round her smoking snout and explained, "The faeries can enchant us to see the best in them, but also the worst in ourselves. If the Queen can divide her enemies, she doesn't need to fight them."

Yann pointed at Lee. "Are you making us argue?"

"No, you're doing it all by yourselves. But your furnace friend might be right, perhaps the Faery Queen is poisoning your friendship."

"Then the sooner we drive her away, the better," muttered Sylvie.

"The sooner we give her what she wants, the better," corrected Helen.

"No! I will not let your mistakes destroy my forest!" growled Sylvie.

Sapphire gave a warning hiss of steam. They were all silent for a moment, staring in embarrassment at the ground.

Then Yann held up his hands. "Let's start again. If we're going to save Helen from this unfortunate bargain, our first task is to steal the flag. We have to plan, so we need privacy." He folded his arms and looked at Lee, clearly waiting for the faery to leave.

Lee grinned at him. "I could help you get the flag."

"How? If faeries could get the flag, you would have got it years ago," Yann sneered.

"And why would you help us get the better of your Queen in a bargain?" Sylvie snarled.

"I can help because I know what has failed before, and I'll explain *why* I want to help if you will listen to my story with open minds. Will you listen?"

Helen would rather hear a story than more arguments. So she sat down. "I'll listen to you, Lee."

Chapter 9

Lee strode to the centre of the circle, his cloak a healthy bright red in the firelight. "Why would I help you get the flag back? That's easy.

"The Fairy Flag is the token of a promise that our faery warriors would fight alongside the MacLeods when they need us most. The flag has the power to summon our army to battle three times. The first time it was waved, we lost dozens of warriors; the second time, we lost hundreds. We don't want to lose thousands if they wave it for a third time. So any faery would help you bring the flag home.

"Why would I help you outwit the Faery Queen? That's harder to explain."

He glanced down at Helen. "You asked me earlier if I was the Faery Queen's subject. I said no, but didn't have time to explain. Now I shall.

"She may summon us to her parties and use her Queen's guard as a small army, but no faery is her subject. I am a loyal and valued subject of … the Faery King," he said grandly.

"There's a Faery King too?" Helen looked around urgently, expecting to see a horde of constantly multiplying magical folk surrounding her.

"Of course! The leader of our armies, the ruler of our lands. He attends her parties sometimes, to be polite, but mostly he sends his supporters and his spies." Lee shrugged. "That's what I am."

Lavender hovered a safe distance away and asked, "You're spying for the Faery King, against the Faery Queen? Why?"

Lee lowered his voice, beckoning his listeners near. "Because my King thinks she's reclaiming her home in this forest in a foolish and dangerous way.

"The Queen has power, but no political sense. These lands were once ours, but time moves on. My King understands that. We can't just come back and steal children, kidnap musicians and drive wolf packs into the open.

"Humans no longer stay out of the forest for fear of wolves or faeries. They come in for fun, with mountain bikes and nature trails. So we can't hunt, fight and dance in the trees as we used to. If we want to stay hidden we must be more subtle. But the Queen is never subtle, so my King has ordered me to prevent her midsummer madness overflowing into the human world.

"Bringing the Fairy Flag back and taking the stolen child home, these will both please my King. That's why I will help you."

Yann snorted. "I don't believe a word you say, faery," he turned to his companions, "and we can't accept help from someone we don't trust."

Sylvie laughed. "It doesn't matter if the story is true or not. Whether he's working for the Queen or the King, he's working for my enemy. That makes *him* my enemy."

Helen disagreed. "Lee has been honest so far. He advised us to feed the boy, then led us to him. I know he didn't help me with the Queen, but neither did anyone else, and Lee did warn me beforehand that he wouldn't be able to do anything. I think we should accept his help."

"You trust a faery?" asked Lavender.

"I believe him when he says he wants the Fairy Flag out of that castle. We can work as a team this time. So, Lee, how do we get the flag?"

Lee arranged the folds of his velvet cloak under him and sat down beside Helen.

"There have been many attempts to free the flag. At first, the MacLeods swaddled every first-born son in the flag, so the bravest of our women applied to be the babes' nurses. The applicants were asked to sing the MacLeod cradle song to soothe the babes to sleep. It's one of our own lullabies, taught to the clan by the faery who married a MacLeod. By the third verse, our women always slipped back into the Faery lyrics rather than the Gaelic, so they were revealed as spies, they didn't get the job, and they didn't get near the flag.

"Since then, my King and his army have tried, almost every midsummer for centuries, to break into Dunvegan. But each chief adds more iron, because they know faeries can't bear to be near iron. Guns on the walls outside, swords on the walls inside, railings on the steps. Every single door and window has so many nails hammered into its frame that the castle must leak like a sieve.

"We can't get in, so we've tried to get the flag out. But neither fire nor famine has ever forced that persistent clan to abandon the castle completely, and they've never taken the flag out unguarded.

"However, they're not guarding against girls, dragons, centaurs, wolves or teeny tiny tasty petal people." Lee bared his perfect teeth at Lavender.

Helen held out her hand to the trembling little fairy, frowning at Lee. "It can't be that simple. The castle is a museum, there must be ancient weapons, fancy portraits, even gold and silver on display. They won't just be guarding against faeries, they must be guarding against human criminals too, with burglar alarms and locks."

"You claimed it would be easy!" Sylvie sneered.

Lee shrugged. "These are human defences. If you want the boy, you must beat them."

Yann said, "Lavender may be small in size, but she is wise beyond her years. Lavender, can you get past these human inventions?"

Lavender nodded. "Simple spells will open most locks that defeat this iron-sick boy, but I'm not so sure about burglar alarms. My people don't make a habit of theft."

Helen said cautiously, "If we find the flag fast and get out quick, perhaps an alarm going off won't be a problem. The police can't arrest a dragon flying over the sea."

Yann said, "If it's speed you want rather than subtlety, I can kick our way in."

Sylvie added, "My teeth can hold off anyone who responds to an alarm."

The wolf girl and the centaur grinned at each other, their earlier argument forgotten in their shared enthusiasm for a fight.

Sapphire creaked a comment. Lavender explained, "Sapphire can find Skye – it's almost due west of this glen and it's the biggest island off the coast – but she's never been to Dunvegan."

Lee said, "I can guide you there. All faeries are drawn to Dunvegan by the flag's power, then repelled by the ring of iron. So you do need my help!"

"Can we all fit on Sapphire?" wondered Helen. "I know she's grown, but there are a lot of us."

Yann frowned. "I won't even try. I will fly on a dragon in an emergency, but it's not really safe for either of us. Sapphire can't manoeuvre well with my weight on her and my legs don't grip like yours. I'll gallop through the mountains to the coast, cross the bridge in the quiet hours of the early morning and meet you in the north of Skye at the first fall of dark tomorrow night."

"Tomorrow night?" objected Helen. "We can't leave this quest until tomorrow! I have to give her the flag tomorrow, so we must fetch it tonight."

Yann shook his head. "If we get it tonight, that cheating Queen will have a night and a day to steal it from you without fulfilling her part of the bargain, just like she's stealing the flag from the MacLeods without fulfilling the third part of the faery promise.

"We have to be in and out fast anyway, so if we break

into the castle as soon as it's dark tomorrow, you can be back at Dorry Shee well before dawn.

"Anyway, you didn't get much sleep last night, my human friend, except when you were pretending to snooze to fool the Wild Hunt. You need a good night's sleep to be sharp for tomorrow night's thievery."

Helen sighed. She didn't want to think of this quest as stealing, however much Yann was enjoying being a criminal mastermind.

Yann spoke to Sapphire about a rendezvous on Skye, then trotted over to Helen, grinning at her. "You did a really daft thing, making that bargain. But I'm sure we can find your happy ever after, even if we have to break windows and bend rules on the way." He laughed, his head back, his hooves dancing on the earth, delighted at the idea of chaos and lawbreaking. "And Father sent me here to keep me out of trouble!"

Yann cantered off towards the Skye Bridge. Sapphire left to find the best route to the sea, while Lee headed back to the centre of the forest.

Finally, alone with Sylvie and Lavender, Helen asked the fairy, "Do you want to come back to the lodge with me?"

"No, thanks." Lavender perched on Sylvie's shoulder.

Helen felt a tiny flutter of jealousy. "I'll just go to bed then, like Yann suggested."

She turned to leave the clearing, but Sylvie kicked earth over the flames and followed her.

"It's nearly full summer dark. We'll walk you home." Sylvie said softly.

"Are you afraid the Wild Hunt will find me tonight?" asked Helen.

Sylvie looked up as they left the trees. Dark grey clouds hid the stars. "There are no hunters in the sky tonight, but we'll walk you home anyway. Humans can't see properly in the dark and you can't smell anything more delicate than dung or roses. You'd be like a baby crawling along a cliff, out in the dark on your own."

"Hardly," said Helen gruffly. "I managed alright last night."

"Nevertheless," insisted Sylvie, "we will come with you."

So Helen chatted to Lavender about places and people they both knew in the Borders, then she tried to include Sylvie in the conversation.

"Sylvie, are you trying to prevent the faery invasion all on your own? Why aren't older wolves fighting the faeries too?"

"I'm never on my own; wolves work as a pack. My brothers are trying to drive the faeries out too, but they're content to let me lead. Our elders ..." she snorted, "they don't use this forest as much as the young wolves. They think diplomacy and tradition will keep the faeries in check, and they hope the faeries will only visit occasionally.

"But I don't think the Queen would go to all this trouble for a holiday home. She's coming back to stay and she'll want more land than this. So while our elders rest their old paws, my brothers and I will defend all our lands, not just this forest."

As they walked along the edge of the trees, their way lit by gentle light from the fairy's wand, Helen saw Sylvie holding her arm.

"Do you want me to bandage that again?"

Sylvie hunched her shoulders and looked up at Helen through her tangled hair.

"Would you? I know it's annoying that I keep shifting and letting it fall off…"

"Of course I'll do it again. Who are you going to be for the rest of tonight? A girl or a wolf?"

Sylvie sniffed the air. "A wolf."

"Then change into a wolf now," instructed Helen. "I'll bandage your leg rather than your arm."

She took her equipment out of the rucksack, as Sylvie's flickering greys shifted at the edge of her vision.

Helen remembered a promise she'd made to phone her mum if she was ever treating an animal on her own again. She sighed. There was no mobile phone reception here, and her mum didn't have any experience with fabled beasts anyway. But it was yet another broken promise.

She examined Sylvie's wound, Lavender hovering close with a circle of light balls. Helen had unpacked a razor, in case she needed to shave a patch of wolf hair, but when she parted the fur and looked closely at the wound, it was clean. Unfortunately, it was also still open, not drawing together or scabbing at all.

"Do you and your pack usually shapeshift when you're injured?" she asked the sharp wolf face. "How do cuts heal if your constant shifting means the wound keeps reopening?"

Sylvie yipped gently and Lavender nodded her head. "Normally, she would stay in the wounded form for at least two days to let healing begin, but in these dangerous times it's more important to be adaptable than to heal the pain in her arm."

Sylvie lifted her muzzle and howled very softly. Lavender shook her head disapprovingly. "She says she will suffer gladly, if her sacrifice will save the forest."

"Nonsense," tutted Helen. "An infection in your arm won't send the Faery Queen home. You need to decide now, Sylvie, would you rather be a wolf or a girl for the next day or so?"

Sylvie grunted a question, which Lavender repeated. "What would be more use in our quest for the flag?"

"I'm glad you agree it's *our* quest! If we need someone girl-shaped, we have me. If we need someone wolf-shaped, only you will do. So I'll bandage this wolf leg, but you must stay a wolf for the next day at least."

She beckoned to Lavender, stood up and whispered to the fairy, "Are you safe with her as a wolf?"

There was a bark of laughter from the sharp-eared wolf below. Lavender smiled. "Wolf people don't eat fairies!" She landed on Sylvie's head. "Sylvie says there's not enough meat on me, so I'm quite safe. Much safer than with great clumping humans obsessed with tooth fairies and wishes."

So Helen knelt down to treat the wolf leg. First she cleaned it, then peered at the labels on various tubes and bottles in the glittering light. Dropping the anaesthetic and arnica creams back into the rucksack, she opened the antiseptic cream. "I'm sure it's not infected, but I'll put this on just in case." Then she placed a soft pad over the wound, wrapped a bandage just above the knobbly knee joint and taped it tidily together. "Run off for a minute then come back and we'll see how secure it is."

She watched as the wolf stretched away into the shadows at a smooth sprint, hardly limping at all. The perfect hunter. After only a few breaths, Sylvie sliced back into the circle of light from the other direction. The neat bandage gleamed white in the fairy light. So did the wolf's grinning teeth. Helen didn't need anyone to translate the soft growl of thanks.

She guessed that Sylvie had insisted on walking with her because she was hoping for a new bandage, so she said, "I'll be fine walking home from here. I'll see you both at the beech tree tomorrow."

With a very light hand, she stroked the soft fur between Sylvie's ears. The wolf sat still and allowed the touch. Helen grinned. Then she said a brief goodbye to Lavender and walked back towards the lodge.

The path was very dark, with no stars, no dragon fire, no fairy light balls to brighten her way. She was wondering if there was a torch in the Murray Wing kitchen, when suddenly she felt a prickle on her neck.

She whirled round. There was nothing there.

She whirled the other way. Wolf eyes, green and sharp and bright, blinked out of sight.

Helen smiled. Sylvie was making sure she got home safely.

She walked on towards the lodge, but as she reached the grey stone building, she thought, surely Sylvie's eyes are gold, not green. And her eyes aren't that big.

Had that been a different wolf? A bigger wolf?

Helen turned and faced the forest. She didn't see anything in the darkness. So she kept on walking, towards her bed, towards as many torches as she could find. Perhaps she shouldn't go out alone in the dark again.

Chapter 10

Helen jerked awake when her alarm blared at 6 am.

Why had she set it so early? What did she need to do at this time in the morning? She couldn't hunt for torches or make sandwiches yet.

Then she saw her violin case on the chair. Of course. She'd set her alarm early so she could rehearse. She hadn't done nearly enough practising since she arrived here to be sure of winning the solo spot.

She picked up her fiddle case and went out to the barn, where she could play as loudly as she liked without disturbing anyone.

The sky was bright. The sun had been up for a couple of hours already. Helen yawned. Why didn't adventures allow more time for sleep?

She closed the big doors behind her.

The new glass roof let in the early sunlight, so Helen could see oddly-shaped heaps scattered about the barn.

The barn was being renovated too, but it wasn't being turned into accommodation. It was becoming a Visitor Centre: The Dorry Shee Experience.

There were piles of dusty rubble, old floorboards, coils of wire and animal feed sacks full of half-bricks at the back of the barn. By the door, protected by polythene sheets, were display boards with pictures of clan tartans, burning crofts and standing stones. Helen saw one display board headed "Local Legends" with cartoon kelpies and selkies, and a portrait of a faery queen dressed in simple green. Helen stepped closer, to see if the faery's face was familiar, then gasped.

Behind the display boards was a collection of stuffed animals. She could see a wolf, a bear, a boar and an eagle, all staring up at her from under plastic covers.

She backed away to the middle of the barn, laid her fiddle case on a toolbox, and opened it. The varnished wood of her fiddle was shinier and more beautiful than any of Lee's green silks or red velvets.

She undid the Velcro straps that held it safe in its case. She reached out for the fiddle, but stopped.

Her stomach lurched at the thought of touching her violin.

If she never touched her violin again, no one would want to steal her away, no one would follow her in the night. If she never played her violin again, she wouldn't be a prize for faeries, nor a threat to wolves.

All this danger and fear was being caused by her music.

She heard a crow call outside. The world was waking

up. She hadn't much time. If she wanted to play her best, then she had to grasp the violin now.

She stroked the satin varnish. It felt familiar and safe.

She lifted out her violin and stood up. Her stomach settled. She was just hungry. She needed her breakfast.

But first she needed to rehearse.

As soon as she began the introduction to Professor Greenhill's dance, she knew this was the right thing to do. Music was meant to be played. And any audience was worth playing for, especially an audience so keen it would cheat and steal to hear your music.

Helen played and played, imagining the Faery Queen's dress swirling wildly in the shadows of the barn.

After a hurried breakfast, a loud and chaotic class on rhythm with a visiting drummer from Cornwall, and a quiet thoughtful lunch, Helen had a free hour before the first full rehearsal.

So she hunted for a torch in the Murray Wing kitchen. She didn't find one, but she did make a quick batch of crust-less jam sandwiches. Then she went to the old lodge and gently removed a map of the Inner Hebrides, including Skye, from the corridor wall. She took a moment to search through the cardboard boxes for something she had glimpsed yesterday. But she still hadn't found a torch.

Rather than searching the rest of the lodge, she went to the cottage, to ask James's mum if she could borrow one.

As Mrs McGregor got a torch out of her toolbox, Helen smiled at the boy, who was sitting still on the couch, looking unconvincing and stiff in a pair of jeans and a tartan shirt. He smiled gloriously back, but didn't move. Emma bounced off the couch and hugged her new friend. "Will you play with me? James isn't playing today."

"Sorry, I can't. I've got a rehearsal, but I'll play with you later, Emma. And I'm sure James will play with you very soon too!"

After thanking Mrs McGregor for the loan of a small silver torch, Helen ran back towards the lodge, carrying the map, some papers, the fiddle case, the sandwiches and the torch, hoping to dump everything but the fiddle in her room before rehearsal. But Professor Greenhill was standing outside the barn, chatting to Dr Lermontov, right in Helen's way.

"What a rush, Helen. And in the wrong direction." The Professor held out a hand to stop her. "And carrying so many things!"

Helen tried to hide the torch in her pocket, as it seemed the most suspicious of all her baggage, but the Professor bumped her arm accidentally and everything fell to the ground.

Dr Lermontov helped Helen pick up the sandwiches and the map. "Were you planning a midnight feast? Or a day trip to the islands? Or some other distraction from your music?"

Professor Greenhill laughed, "I hope you *are* finding distractions, my dear girl."

Dr Lermontov frowned.

"A bit of distraction is a good thing for an artist," the Professor explained. "It doesn't do to concentrate on just one thing, does it, Helen?"

Helen was about to ask what that meant, when suddenly there was a gust of cold wind. The Professor pulled her scarf over her head and ran to the lodge, tottering on her pointy green shoes. Dr Lermontov dragged Helen and her collection of quest equipment straight to the rehearsal.

The only building on the estate big enough for a full rehearsal was the barn. Some students made faces at the dusty floor and Tommy had to be dissuaded from using the boar's back as a drum, but perhaps Dr Lermontov had been right yesterday. Perhaps it really didn't matter where they performed, because in that barn the twenty students played together so perfectly that it sounded to Helen like they'd played together all their lives.

They were soaring to the end of the last movement when the Professor bounced in, applauding and telling them they were the greatest young musicians she'd ever heard.

She went into a huddle with Dr Lermontov, then they called out two cellists. One was Alice, from Helen's wing, the other was Stewart, a large boy from Galloway. They were both asked to play part of the last movement. Alice was clearly nervous and, at the slowest part of the andante section, her bow quivered on the D string and the cello let out a short screeching howl. Alice recovered and kept on playing, but the shock of the howl echoed round the barn.

Juliet caught Helen's eye and mouthed, "Wolf note?" Helen grimaced and nodded.

It didn't take a very long huddle for Professor Greenhill to announce that Stewart would play a solo on midsummer night.

Helen was suddenly worried. She hadn't realized Professor Greenhill would consult Dr Lermontov about soloists. But why wouldn't she? He was her deputy. Helen was kicking herself for not behaving better in the Russian's lesson yesterday. Why had she been thinking about faery mounds, rather than concentrating on her music?

Dr Lermontov thought she was strange, for goodness sake. He would never want her as a soloist.

She held her breath as he said, "Now we will hear a few of our violinists.

"Zoe Quarrier, step to the front."

Helen bit her lip.

"Calum McIvor, you too."

Helen went cold with disappointment and anger. They weren't even going to consider her! Then she heard:

"And Helen Strang-ah.

"Let's hear you all. Play the violin solo from the second movement."

Helen nodded. At least she was getting to audition. She stood nervously as the older players got ready, wondering if their extra years of experience would help them perform better.

Zoe began to play.

Helen knew her rival was a good violinist, but now she heard how great Zoe could be on her own. Freed from the compromises of playing with others, Zoe got amazing speed and volume out of her bow. But at the end of the section, when the music became subtler and dreamier, Zoe simply slowed and quietened, without finding any depth. Helen relaxed a little. The great Zoe was only noise and passion, not understanding.

Then Calum played. He hit each note with perfection, but also played each note with exactly the same weight as the one before and the one after. Soon, though the music was wonderful, his playing sounded dull and mechanical.

Then it was Helen's turn.

She was sure if she played at her best, she could play better than either Zoe or Calum, but her fingers and shoulders were stiff with tension. Helen took her time. She rolled her shoulders, shook out her hands one at a time and balanced carefully on her feet.

Then she rested her fiddle on her shoulder, held her bow gently in her right hand, and breathed in time to the music she could already hear in her head.

She played to the Professor who had created this music, to the musicians in the past who had inspired it, to the audiences in the future who would lose their hearts to it. She played with light and dark, with love and fear, with notes dancing around her hands.

She played brilliantly. She allowed herself one small smile as she lowered her bow at the end.

The Professor and the Doctor went into a long huddle in the far corner of the barn, with lots of muttering and head shaking.

Then the Professor smiled kindly at all three nervous violinists. "You were all so wonderful we can't decide just now. You are each capable of being our soloist, so just keep practising and we'll let you know before midsummer night."

Zoe burst out, "That's not fair! You can't keep us waiting!"

Helen was afraid to nod, but she agreed with Zoe.

Dr Lermontov laughed uncomfortably. "It's all part of learning to be great musicians, I'm afraid. Not just disappointment, like those behind you who didn't even get the chance, but also uncertainty, like the three of you will suffer until the Professor makes up her mind."

So, thought Helen, he's already made up his mind who was best. Not me, probably, because I don't concentrate on theory. Helen shrugged. There was no point trying to read adults' minds. It was harder than trying to outwit faeries.

Professor Greenhill patted Zoe on the shoulder. "What a great problem for me to have! So many wonderful fiddlers!" She gave all three possible soloists a small neat smile, then wafted out of the barn on her shiny green heels.

Zoe turned to Helen and hissed, "I said the solo spot was mine. How dare you play so well!"

Helen grinned. "That wasn't me playing well. That was me playing like my little sister, to give you a chance!"

Zoe glared at her. Helen stepped quickly into the safety of the rest of the students, several of whom whispered that she had played the other two out of the barn and it was a disgrace she hadn't been chosen.

Dr Lermontov tapped his dusty toes sharply on the barn floor to get everyone's attention. "It's nearly teatime, so I'm afraid the woodwind and percussion players will have to wait until tomorrow for their solo competitions. Why don't you all go and clean your instruments before eating."

Then he bent down to clean his own shoes with a spotty red hankie. Helen thought the Professor must have found a swept bit of floor in the far corner, leaving her deputy standing in the rubble, because the Professor's shoes had been pristine as she teetered out of the barn.

Helen ate a pleasant tea in a very unpleasant atmosphere. Zoe wanted everyone to agree it was unfair she hadn't been chosen as the soloist. The students at their table tried to soothe her by agreeing it was stressful not to know, but they wouldn't comment on who should have been chosen.

Zoe wouldn't take a hint. "They're not going to choose a snotty little kid! She only played half decently because she copied everything I did. They probably didn't pick me straight away because they were worried she would throw a toddler tantrum."

Juliet finally said, "Shut up, Zoe. Helen might be a snotty-nosed kid, but she's handling the strain of top level playing much better than you are."

Zoe shoved her chair back and stomped out of the dining room. Now everyone at the table stared at Helen.

Juliet said, "Sorry. I don't mean you're a snotty-nosed kid. I just mean … for someone so young …"

Catriona, the piper who slept in the fifth bed in Murray Wing, said, "After pudding, do you want to watch a DVD with us, in one of the boys' wings?"

Helen looked round at the faces smiling at her. She didn't know if they wanted to be her friends because she was a good fiddler, because she wasn't Zoe, or because they actually liked her. Whatever their reason, she couldn't stay any longer.

y. I'd love to, but I need to get some fresh air."

ona shrugged. "Fair enough." The teenagers started to chat among themselves.

Helen left the dining room through the door into Murray Wing. As she reached the top of the stairs, she heard sobbing from along the corridor. From Zoe's room. Helen sighed and opened her own bedroom door.

She packed everything she'd found today into her pockets and the rucksack, and walked back down the stairs. She wasn't sneaking away, because the others knew she was going for a walk, but a green rucksack with a white cross on it might be hard to explain, so she headed for the side door, rather than the door leading into the old lodge.

First she wrote on the clipboard: Out for a walk, in big dark letters, then in pale small handwriting under it: Early night again. With any luck by the time the teachers checked at bedtime, they would assume she had come back in and gone to bed.

Walking through the bright evening to the dark forest, Helen's shoulders relaxed. She knew who she was with the fabled beasts. None of them needed to prove themselves with a solo; they all played completely different parts.

She strode along the path, whistling the last movement of Professor Greenhill's composition.

As she concentrated on the tempo, and on mixing other people's parts with her own, she didn't see the lean bodies creeping along beside her just inside the forest edge, flashes of ash, steel and black fur showing through gaps in the trees.

She stepped into the clearing, whistling the last few

bars. As she pulled the music up through its crescendo, she saw Lee staring at her, his eyes blazing, his right arm wrapped round the broad trunk of the beech tree as if he was trying to stop himself leaping off a cliff. His cloak was fluorescent and his boots were twitching on the ground.

Helen stopped whistling abruptly.

Lavender swooped down to her. "Don't whistle that. Not here."

"Why not?"

"You don't want to draw the faeries' attention with that music. Not any music."

Helen looked around. Lee was now leaning calmly against the tree. Sylvie was lying, paws loose, on the ground. Lavender was bobbing in the air in front of her. "Where's Sapphire?"

"A few minutes west of here," the fairy said. "She can't take off from the edge of the forest before darkness falls; it's too close to your lodge. We'll walk to her."

Sylvie leapt enthusiastically to her paws, with no sign of a limp, though the bandage was still secure on her front leg. She smiled toothily at Helen.

Helen wanted to smile back, to build a stronger friendship with the wolf, but she couldn't forget the eyes she'd seen last night.

"Sylvie, after I bandaged your leg, did you follow me home?"

Sylvie shook her pale grey head.

"Then why did I see wolf's eyes behind me?"

Sylvie didn't answer.

"Who was following me, Sylvie?"

Sylvie still didn't answer; now she wasn't meeting Helen's eyes.

Lavender said sternly, "Sylvie, are your brothers stalking Helen?"

Sylvie snarled.

Lavender pointed her wand at the wolf's snout. "You fools! That's the fastest way to force a human into the arms of the faeries! With a wolf pack behind and a faery mound ahead, what do you think a human child will choose?

"Call your brothers off, Sylvie, or you'll get no more help from me or Helen."

Sylvie growled at her.

Lavender raised her tiny voice. "Of course we're helping! And you can't do this yourself! One pack of wolves, against all the faeries at the King's command? You know you would lose. But Helen has a skill the faeries value; she has a power over them that none of us have. Work with her and you might just win."

Sylvie barked and grunted, then stalked off to the edge of the clearing and started scratching her sides dismissively.

Lavender turned to Helen. "Sylvie is worried that we're trying to save the child and the musicians, but not her forest. That we'll fetch the faeries' treasure for them, but not drive them away. She won't call her brothers off, but she will keep them at a distance for as long as she thinks we have a chance of defeating the Queen."

Helen shivered at the thought of walking through the forest with a pack of wolves watching her. "Do her brothers listen to her? Will they keep their distance if she tells them to?"

Lavender laughed. "Yes, they listen to Sylvie, if they don't want chewed ears and bitten muzzles! The alpha wolf in a pack is not always the biggest male. It can be the cleverest, fastest female." She spoke as loudly as she could, and Helen saw Sylvie's hackles relax as she heard her friend's description of her.

So Sylvie led the way towards Sapphire, with Lavender fluttering above her head.

Lee and Helen followed, along paths edged by bushes heavy with blaeberries and the long stems of buttercups. Lee walked slower than usual, so they fell behind, losing sight of the wolf's high waving tail.

"Lee, what's making you nervous?" asked Helen.

"I'm not nervous."

"Yes, you are. Your waistcoat was decorated with peacocks when we left the clearing, now it's covered in flocks of crows! Are you nervous about the castle?"

"No."

"The dragon flight?"

"No!"

"What then?"

Lee sighed. "I'm about to step out of my world into yours, to take a human's side in a faery bargain. The Queen will not be forgiving if she finds out. But my King said I must help you, so that's what I'll do." He made an effort to smile. "However it affects my waistcoats!"

"Your King said you had to help *me!* Me specifically? He had heard of me?"

"Yes, he has heard of the healer's child and bard, and he doesn't want you to fall into the Queen's hands."

"Does *he* like music?" Helen asked lightly, wondering if it was safer to play for the King than the Queen.

"He loves music." Lee looked at her seriously. "He

loves it, though he can usually control his greed for it. But it wouldn't be wise to tempt him. Or me." He walked off, his steps fast and determined again.

Helen remembered the look on Lee's face when she had been whistling and kept quiet for the rest of the walk.

They came out of the trees on the northern side of a small hill, where Sapphire's take-off would be hidden from the summer school. Sylvie and Lavender were already on the dragon ... and they were all laughing.

The fairy's giggles, the wolf's howls and the dragon's snorts were getting hysterical, as they tried to stop the wolf's hairy legs and clicking claws slipping down the dragon. Sapphire kept extending her wings to catch Sylvie as she slithered off.

Helen laughed too as she climbed up. She sat behind the wolf, wrapping her arms round the hairy ribcage to hold Sylvie steady. Then she used one hand to hold onto a silver spike and her legs to grip the dragon's scaly sides. Lavender settled on her shoulder. Lee climbed up behind her.

"Anyone want me to sing 'Over the Sea to Skye?'" Helen called as Sapphire took off, then laughed as everyone, including the faery behind her, yelled back, "No!"

Chapter 11

Dunvegan Castle loomed over Helen as she got ready to break the law.

Not a magical law.

Not a school rule, nor a family rule.

But the law. The law that says you don't break into other people's homes and steal from them.

Why was she doing this? To save a small boy she hardly knew? To save herself from playing music she loved, to an audience that would really appreciate it?

"Second thoughts, healer's child?" asked Yann. He'd been waiting for the dragon and her passengers on the beach under the towered and turreted castle.

For all its fancy bits, Dunvegan didn't look like a fairytale palace, nor a rich man's mansion. Dunvegan was a fortress, built to fend off other clans and interfering Scottish kings, as well as faeries.

"Second thoughts?" Yann repeated.

"No. Let's go."

The first and strongest defence was the high sheer rock on which the castle was built, with a stone wall all round. If you didn't want to approach the solid front door over its narrow bridge, you had to scale the cliff at the back. And if you didn't have the key to the small gate in the outer wall, you were left clinging to the hard rock, above a stony, seaweed-slippy beach.

The rock had defeated the MacLeods' rivals, the MacDonalds, for centuries. But the MacDonalds had never arrived by dragon.

Sapphire took only four beats of her huge wings to lift Yann up and over the wall. Then she came back down for Helen, Lavender, Sylvie and Lee.

They landed on a grassy space overlooked on three sides by the tall walls of the castle, its long narrow windows and its high square towers. Behind them was the defensive wall, cut low in places to hold the cannon that still pointed outwards, guarding against attacking ships.

But the three sides of the castle didn't box them in; the walls weren't built at right angles. They opened at the wide angle of a stage set or a soaring bird's wings. The glow from Sapphire's throat gave the smooth brown walls a golden sheen.

There was only one door from this gun-court into the back of the castle, an ordinary black back door, leading into a modern extension built against the castle wall to their left. The extension was just one storey high. A narrow staircase with railings led up from the gun-court to its flat roof.

"That way," Helen pointed. "If we go up that staircase, across the roof and through that middle window into the drawing room, we'll be right beside the flag."

Lavender looked astonished. "Do you have a finding spell, human girl?"

"No!" Helen laughed softly. "I have the guidebook! There's a big box of Skye tourist information in the lodge." She pulled a glossy booklet from her pocket.

Yann took charge. "Sapphire will stay here on guard. The rest of us will make our way to the window Helen has identified. If it's locked, Lavender will open it using her gentle magic. If that doesn't work, I'll kick it in. We go in, grab the flag and get out as fast as possible. Sapphire will fly all of you to Dorry Shee and I'll come back overnight."

Yann strode towards the staircase, elegant, powerful and completely in command of this quest. He looked a little less commanding when the width of his horse chest got stuck in the slim gap between the iron railings before his hooves had climbed up the first step.

He backed away, not meeting anyone's eye, letting Helen climb up instead. Sylvie trotted on her silent paws at Helen's heels. Lavender flew straight to the window.

Yann took a few steps back. Helen wondered if there was space for him to get up enough speed to jump onto the roof. Then she noticed Lee standing miserably on the grass, halfway between the dragon and the staircase. "Lee," she whispered loudly, "aren't you coming up?"

He pointed at the black metal railings. "I can't fit myself between those iron spears any more than the horse can."

Yann muttered something under his breath, then trotted over to Lee.

Yann bent his head down, Lee tipped his face up and there was a short conversation. Neither boy looked happy about it, but they must have reached an agreement, because Lee pulled himself up onto Yann's back and put his arms round Yann's waist, while Yann stood tensely still, like Helen's little sister trying not to squeal when a bee buzzed round her. *They really don't like each other,* Helen thought.

Yann backed right up to the cannon in the wall and burst into a sudden gallop, thundering straight for the back door. Halfway there, he pushed off the ground and launched into the air in a smooth curve. The roof creaked as his weight hit.

Lee slid off Yann's back almost before all four hooves were on the roof. He bowed low, wafting his cloak in a curve as smooth as the centaur's leap. "Thank you, noble steed."

Yann grunted. They moved as far from each other as the narrow space allowed.

Lavender was flying slowly round the window. Sylvie was on her hind legs, sniffing around the frame.

Lavender said, "The window has faded magical protections which I could sneeze away and an ordinary human latch that I can open with a bit of effort."

Sylvie yipped. Yann turned to Helen. "There are scents of many humans in the room, but Sylvie doesn't think there are any hot smells. She thinks we're safe, but she can't guarantee it."

Helen nodded. "There must have been busloads of summer tourists through that room today. I'm sure it'll be empty now, so let's get going."

Lavender hovered in front of the window, drawing the shape of each pane with her wand. Her hand was moving fast when she started at the top, then got slower and heavier, as she worked her way down. Finally she sat, exhausted, on the sill. The window was still shut.

Lee snorted from the edge of the roof. "Can't you open it? So much for your wiser ways!"

Lavender smiled. "I'm far too wise to do the heavy lifting. That's what I have centaurs and humans for. I've unlocked it. Someone else can open it."

Helen dashed forward, worried Yann would be tempted to use his hooves. She shifted the tired Lavender to the next window sill, then grasped the bottom of the window. She jerked it upwards, sliding the lower half of the window smoothly behind the top half. Sylvie leapt in, grey fur brushing against Helen, and immediately started sniffing around.

Helen climbed over the sill and Yann handed Lavender to her. He shook his head when Helen invited him in. "The gap is too small," he pointed out, "but I will be just out here. If you need me inside, I can kick the top panes away."

"No," she whispered. "We need to be quiet." She looked past him at Lee. The faery put his hands on the stone sill, leaning forward to put his head through the gap.

The nearer his face got to the space inside the window frame, the slower he moved. By the time his face was almost in the room, Helen could see the skin pressing against his skull, like he was pushing his flesh against glass rather than air.

He tried three times, then took a wobbly step back, shaking his head, his eyes watering, his skin grey.

"Iron," he gasped. "Nails in the frame. I can feel them. Dozens of them. It was built to keep me out. I just can't get in."

Yann looked at him with contempt. "Does it hurt, Lily? Is that what's stopping you?"

Lee laughed. "Yes, it hurts. But even if I was prepared to walk through fire, with splinters up my fingernails and skewers in my chest, I couldn't get past it."

"Coward! You should always fight past pain."

"Could you jump to the top of that tower," Lee pointed five or six storeys above them, "just by ignoring the pain in your legs from the speed it would need?"

Yann shook his head reluctantly.

"Then believe me, it's not fear of pain that's stopping me. I just can't get through it. It is a wall built to keep me out; dogs and flowers and children can skip through it, but I can't."

He looked at Helen. "Be careful in there, girl, the defences may not end at the window." Then he staggered to the corner of the roof, far from the window frame and the iron railings, and sat down, head in his hands, shoulders slumped.

Helen turned and walked into the room. Sylvie was nosing round the skirting boards, and Lavender was casting balls of light up to the ceiling.

It was surprisingly pink. A drawing room, the guidebook said. With a fancy rug, deep pink armchairs, and little varnished tables. Helen had expected swords on walls, shields over doors and possibly roast ox in the fireplace. Instead the fireplace was filled with dried flowers. Surely there couldn't be any danger in such a girly room.

A sudden groaning roar erupted from the doorway to her left. Helen jumped back, but when Sylvie rushed forward, Helen followed at her tail.

She didn't know what she expected to see. Clan warriors yelling a war cry as they defended their ancestral banner? A mythical monster patrolling the castle? If it was either of those things, why was she running towards it?

Sylvie streaked ahead. Lavender followed, throwing white light balls so fast they trailed glitter in the air. They found themselves in a small corridor. Empty. Silent. It filled again with a horrendous eerie groan.

Sylvie was growling, ears flat to her head, raised fur sharp on her high haunches. Lavender was spiralling in the air, trying to find an enemy.

Helen stood still and looked around carefully. She saw a sign by an opening in the wall:

> Dungeon. This dungeon was dug out of the living rock when the castle was built. The clan chiefs threw enemies and thieves into the pit and left them here to starve. We can only imagine their groans of despair as food smells from the kitchen reached their nostrils through the tiny window cut into their dark cell.

She glanced in through the dungeon doorway. A metal grille covered a hole in the stone floor. A crumpled pile of clothes at the bottom of the stone pit must represent a prisoner in despair. A loudspeaker just above her head let out another groan.

She laughed. "It's just sound effects for tourists. Not a warrior or a monster."

They headed back towards the drawing room, Sylvie's tail curving between her legs.

Helen glanced quickly round the room. She wondered if it had been this pink when real prisoners were starving just yards from its fireplace. She wondered what the thieves had been imprisoned for stealing. She shivered, then checked the room's layout against the diagrams in the guidebook.

There were two main doors, one leading to the dungeon and one in the opposite corner leading to the castle's grand staircase.

There was also a narrow doorway, in the corner beyond the pink chairs. It might lead to the kitchen, she thought, if food smells tantalized the prisoners. Another low door was hidden behind a grand piano in the fourth corner. Perhaps it was a cupboard.

They were alone, in a well-lit room, with a safe exit out of the window and only the groans from the dungeon to disturb them.

It was safe to steal the Fairy Flag.

But at first Helen couldn't find it.

She knew it was hanging on the wall beside the open window. It was marked with an X on the map in the guidebook. She'd expected to find a banner, hanging from a lance, fringes wafting gently in the breeze from the sea.

Instead, beside the window, the glare from Lavender's defensively bright light was bouncing off the glass of a large framed picture. Helen walked past it, assuming it was a portrait of an elderly clan chief. When she realized there was no fabric hanging anywhere else in the room, she went back to the picture, shooed Lavender's light balls away and glimpsed a creamy shape behind the glass.

A ragged sketch of a banner. A thin yellowy piece of material, dotted with red stitches and uneven holes, crushed under glass to stop the breath of tourists wearing it away.

There was a wooden table under the picture frame, piled with laminated cards describing the legends of the Fairy Flag in English, French, German and Japanese. Helen put the cards on the floor and scrambled onto the table. It wobbled, but didn't break. She reached as high as she could to lift the flag from the pair of hooks holding it to the wall.

She turned round, with the awkward sharp-cornered frame in her arms. It was surprisingly heavy. She couldn't jump down holding it and she couldn't drop it to the floor. She glanced at her companions. Sylvie's paws couldn't grasp the frame and Lavender was too small even to get her hands round it.

Yann peered in and saw Helen teetering on the table. He tried to reach in to help, but he couldn't get his torso under the upper half of the window. Before he could smash the panes of glass blocking his way, Sylvie growled at him. Then she pulled cushions off the pink chairs and dragged them in her jaws to the floor below the table.

Helen smiled her thanks to the wolf, dropped the heavy frame onto the soft cushions, then jumped down.

"Should we take it out of the frame?" she asked Sylvie and Lavender.

"Hurry up," called Yann from the window. Helen heard more groans and creaks from outside the room.

But she didn't rush. She examined the flag. "It might fall apart if we take it out, but this frame is going to be hard to carry on Sapphire's back."

She turned the frame over. Now she could see why it was so heavy: metal wire was stretched in a lattice over the back of it.

"We can't give the flag to the Faery Queen with iron all over it and we can't get both Lee and this frame on Sapphire's back. We have to take the flag out. Sylvie, can you hunt for a box or a bag we can carry the flag in?"

Helen opened her first aid kit, found the strongest scalpel, then sliced through the edges of the wire, pulling her hand away as the wires pinged back like sharp elastic bands.

Then she slit through the brown card backing where it met the wooden frame. She turned the whole thing over and started to take it apart layer by layer. The rectangular frame. The huge sheet of glass. Suddenly, there was the Fairy Flag, exposed to the air for the first time in years.

Sylvie trotted back with a small beaded box.

"Perfect. Thanks." Helen replaced the scalpel carefully and slung the rucksack on her back again.

There was another creak, from the narrow door that might lead to the kitchen.

Sylvie growled.

"It's just the sound effects, don't worry." Helen put her hand on the cobweb softness of the flag, wondering whether to fold it or roll it.

Lavender was standing at the very edge of the fabric, peering down at the tiny red darns.

There was another creak.

Sylvie howled.

Helen heard the squeak of doors opening and the thump of feet on floorboards.

But this time, the squeak and the thump weren't sound effects for tourists.

This time, the two narrow doors in the corners of the drawing room swung open and a horde of stocky figures ran in. On hairy feet. Wielding long sharp metal weapons.

Chapter 12

The hairy creatures rushed towards Helen, Sylvie and Lavender, waving their weapons, muttering under their breath.

Sylvie leapt forward to stand between Helen and the creatures. Growling, baring her teeth, snapping at anything that came close.

Helen yanked the flag out of the frame. Lavender fell over as the fabric was pulled from under her feet. Helen crumpled the flag into the box, slammed the beaded lid shut and stood up.

There were dozens of hairy figures, held at armslength by Sylvie's fast moving jaws.

What were they?

They were shaped like small people, clothed in nothing but shaggy brown or grey hair. They had fearsome faces: wide mouths, squinting eyes, huge noses. In their broad hairy hands they clutched ladles, sieves, feather dusters, fish slices, rakes, dish-brushes …

In answer to Sylvie's eerie howls and the dungeon groans, they were barely raising their voices. "Put the flag back. Tidy it up. Put it back."

Helen said firmly, "No, we're taking the flag to its true owners, the faeries."

Yann yelled through the window, "Don't argue, just get out."

So Helen grabbed Lavender off the frame, sat the fairy on her shoulder and took a step towards the window.

As soon as she moved, the hairy horde broke.

They burst past Sylvie, muttering ever louder, "Put the flag back."

Sylvie pounced, knocking a few to the ground, but the rest ran to get between Helen and the window. They didn't attack. They just stood there. Waving their utensils, muttering, "Put the flag back."

"And the cushions," muttered one little figure with long blond hair all over its body. "Tidy the cushions too."

Yann's hooves hit the window with a massive crash, scattering wood, glass and dull iron nails all over the rug and the hairy creatures. Some muttered complaints, most brushed the glass off their hair and one, with a dustpan and brush, started to sweep up.

Yann ordered, "Push through them. They aren't violent. Just get past them, before someone hears this noise."

"What are they?" shouted Helen over the crescendo of muttering, growls and groans.

"They're brownies," said Lavender, "and they *can* be violent, Yann, if pushed hard enough. You know they don't like breakages and mess."

Helen raised the box above her head, higher than the short brownies could reach, and moved towards the mass of hair and noses in her way. She pushed a mop and a garden hose aside.

"Don't provoke them," Lavender advised from Helen's shoulder. "Don't make any more mess. Perhaps we should offer to tidy up …?"

Helen was nearly at the window. Yann was reaching in for her. She could hear Sylvie panting behind her.

Then a dark hairy hand reached out and plucked Lavender from Helen's left shoulder. Another hairy hand grabbed her right sleeve, trying to drag down her arm … and the box.

"Put the flag back," muttered the brownie holding Lavender.

Helen reached out and grabbed hold of the fairy's arm. "Give her back!"

Lavender was squealing as the hairy fingers squeezed her feathery wing.

The dark brownie muttered, "Put the flag back and you get the fairy back. All neat and tidy."

Helen couldn't bring her other arm down to prise Lavender free. Yann was trying to get his front legs over the windowsill.

Helen yelled, "Yann! Take the box, then I can get Lavender back."

She tried to stretch her arm, to give the box to Yann.

Then Sylvie bit the brownie holding Lavender and he jerked. At the same moment, the small blond brownie leapt off a newly built tower of cushions and grabbed the box from Helen. She jerked too. There was a pop and a scream. Lavender fell through the air, as both Helen and the dark brownie let go in shock. Sylvie picked the purple fairy up in her jaws and the blond brownie scrambled off with the box.

Sylvie bounded out of the window carrying Lavender's air-ripping screams with her. Yann leant forward, grabbed Helen and dragged her over the window sill.

Helen whirled round and looked into the pink room. The blond brownie was laying the flag back in the frame, smoothing it flat. Several other brownies were putting the cushions on the chairs, patting them into shape. The one with the feather duster was dusting the table, removing Helen's footprints.

"I can still get it!" She struggled to climb back in as Yann held her by the shoulders. "What will they do to me, tickle me with feathers? Scrub me with a toilet brush?"

"They've ripped Lavender apart," bellowed Yann. "Forget the flag. Your friend needs you."

Then Helen heard another sound over the fairy's screams and the brownies' muttering of "Tidy it up. Put it back. What a mess."

She heard a police siren.

So she scrambled onto Yann's back and clung on as he leapt down to the gun-court. Lee leapt down beside them, his red cloak billowing out like wings.

The noise of the police siren was drowned out by Lavender's screams as they flew north.

"What's wrong?" Helen found herself yelling at the distraught fairy. *"What's wrong with you?"*

Lavender couldn't answer. She just screamed so piercingly, loudly and constantly that Helen could hardly think.

Lee was muttering instructions to Sapphire. Past the screams, Helen had been dimly aware of the faery giving directions to Yann, left behind below the castle, as they took off over the sea.

Now they were flying over tiny dark islands, dotted with the fat wet forms of seals. Suddenly they landed on a glowing white beach.

"Coral beach," Lee said briskly. "Will reflect light. Help you heal her. Easy for Yann to find in the dark." He took a deep breath. "Now please make her stop!"

"But I don't know what's wrong! How can I fix her when I don't know what's wrong?"

Sylvie growled. Lee said, "Animals can't tell you what's wrong, but you and your mother fix them. We know you can do it."

So Helen put her fleece on the rough white sand. Sapphire kindled a fiery light in her throat, while Helen laid the fairy gently on the fleece. On her back. Lavender shrieked even louder. Helen turned her onto her front. The screams lessened slightly.

She looked closely at the fairy's back.

No blood.

No shards of glass sticking out of her tiny body.

What was *wrong?*

"Lee, do you have any healing magic, or any way of calming her down?"

Lee, with his hands over his ears, shook his head. Sylvie was whining, her ears flat to her skull, sliding on her belly further from the piercing squeals.

Helen looked again. Lavender's wings didn't look right. They emerged from her back at slightly different angles.

Oh no.

She remembered the moment she and the brownie had both jerked, playing a brief tug of war with the fairy. She had been holding Lavender's arm; the dark brownie had been holding her wing. They had jerked in different directions.

Oh no.

Lavender's wing was dislocated.

But which wing?

The right and the left wings were lying at different angles, but which was the correct angle and which was the wrong angle?

Helen closed her eyes, trying to remember exactly what had happened. Lavender had been facing forward. Helen had held her right arm, the brownie had held her left wing.

So the left wing was the one at the wrong angle. It had been wrenched out of its socket. To heal her friend and to stop this awful keening noise, Helen had to fit the left wing back in.

How did her mother do this? On an operating table, not a beach. With anaesthetic.

Helen had seen her repair a dislocation on an Alsatian. The dog had been unconscious while her

131

mother manipulated the joint. Helen had held up an x-ray of the injured joint and a diagram of a healthy dog's anatomy. Her mother had kept comparing the two, like doing a jigsaw puzzle while looking at the lid of the box.

Helen felt the fairy's shoulders and the tops of her wings with gentle fingers. She doubted a diagram of fairy anatomy existed anywhere. Where did Lavender's wings connect? Did she have four shoulders? How could Helen put this puzzle back together when she didn't know what the right answer looked like?

She looked up at her companions. All trying hard to stay and support her, but all clearly feeling ill listening to the shrill cries. Even Sapphire's flames were a vomity yellow colour. However, not one of them looked like an expert on fairy anatomy.

What about anaesthetic? Perhaps if the fairy's pain eased, she would stop screaming and Helen could think more clearly.

She found the box of painkiller in the rucksack. She'd used it before, but never on someone as small as Lavender. She studied the recommended doses for different animals, then looked at the size of the needle.

There was no amount of this drug that she could safely administer to a flower fairy. Even a drop might be enough to kill a being as light as Lavender, and sticking her with the needle would be like stabbing her with a sword.

Helen put her head in her hands and groaned.

There was a crunching noise on the coral sand, as Yann slid to a stop behind Sapphire.

"The police have lit the castle up like a bonfire,"

he gasped. "I hope they're arresting all those blasted brownies!" Then he frowned. "Lavender? Are you alright?" He glared at Helen. "Why haven't you healed her yet?"

"I can't! Her wing is dislocated and I don't know how to put it back! If I put it back without anaesthetic, it'll be excruciating. Anyway, I don't know where it needs to go; if I make a mistake, I could cripple her forever!"

"You're our healer. You have to help her!"

"I can't! I don't know what a fairy wing joint is meant to feel like! Do you have a plastic fairy skeleton in your pouch, Yann? A fairy anatomical diagram? I can't work blind. I just can't risk it!"

Sylvie growled. Yann said, "Sylvie knows where there is a perfect wing joint you can examine. If you have that, can you heal her?"

"I can try," mumbled Helen.

"Then feel the other wing!" shouted Yann. "The other wing is fine!"

Helen groaned again. Why hadn't she thought of that? The screams were pounding her brain into pigswill.

Inspired by Sylvie's idea, she had one of her own. The anaesthetic injection was too dangerous, but she took out the anaesthetic cream she had found when treating Sylvie's arm. It was impossible to use too much of this: the dose was limited by the skin area it could touch.

It wouldn't stop the pain completely, but it might dull it enough to stop Lavender screaming any louder.

She pulled Lavender's dress off her shoulders, ripping it slightly. Then she put a tiny drop of cream on her own left pinky, as she didn't want to numb the fingers she needed to force the wing back in, and rubbed a small amount of cream round the joint.

Lavender shrieked even more. Helen sighed. She would have to ignore her friend's screams and pain. She was going to make them worse, before she made them better.

She looked up at her audience. "This will hurt her and she will scream louder. But if I don't do it, she'll be screaming all night and may never fly again. Mind you, if I get it wrong, she may never fly again anyway…" Her voice trailed away, eaten by the screams.

"Sorry, Lavender," she apologised in advance. Then she tuned out the screams and listened to her fingertips.

She ran her fingers along the perfect right wing. The lilac feathers overlapped along the light wing bones: short feathers near the body, longer feathers at the end. The wing was attached to the fairy's body on what seemed to be a second set of shoulder blades, between the spine and the arm joints at the shoulder.

Helen moved the right wing gently. It rotated almost 360 degrees, nearly a full circle, which was why Lavender could fly as fancily as a dragonfly. It slotted into her body just a finger width from the top of her spine. Helen could feel the muscles in the wing push back at her as she moved it, strong and springy.

Then Helen touched the left wing. Lavender made a noise like a loudspeaker with feedback.

The left wing hung limp. When Helen moved it, it shuddered and grated. It looked longer than the right wing, as if the end of the joint was outside the body, not inside.

Helen pulled the wing straight, ignoring Lavender's ever louder screams, barely hearing Sylvie's threatening growls and Yann's cries of "What are you doing to her? Stop! Stop!"

She held the limp wing steady, scraping the end across the tiny inner shoulder blade, prodding and searching for the socket of the joint. If she went the wrong way she would rip all the tendons, maybe even rip the wing off; but she was trying to make it look symmetrical with the other wing, so she hoped she was forcing the bone the correct way.

Scrape. Just a little further. Scrape. Where was it? Scrape. It must be here!

There was a soggy lurch as the wing found a hole … and a click as it slid in.

Lavender screamed even louder and then fell suddenly, appallingly, silent.

Yann screamed now too. A deeper, terrifying yell. "Have you killed her? Human child? Have you killed my friend?"

"No." Helen's fingers were shaking as she tidied the neck of Lavender's ripped dress. "She's fainted. I think I got it back in." She peered down. "It looks right. At least she's stopped screaming!"

"Give her to me!" demanded Yann. "I want to hear her breathe!"

Helen stood up and handed the limp fairy to Yann. He cradled her in his hands.

"I felt her shiver. She is still alive!"

He looked at Helen. "Sorry. I thought you'd killed her. That was a very brave thing to do, to try something you had never done before, with all that noise and with us watching. You are a true healer. Not just a healer's child."

"Let's see if she can fly when she wakes up," Helen said quietly.

"I'll hear that scream in my dreams," moaned Lee, wobbling his forefingers in his ears. "Well done for quietening her."

Then he took his fingers out of his ears and smiled his glorious smile. "And well done for getting the flag."

There was silence. Total silence, now there was no screaming.

"You did get the flag? Those soft hairy housework faeries didn't scare you into giving it to them?"

Helen hung her head. "I couldn't keep hold of it. They put it back." She looked up at his disappointed face. "I'm sorry, Lee. I didn't get your flag."

Lee looked away. "Don't apologise to me. But you'd better start thinking of an apology for the Queen. Healer you may be, but perhaps you're not a true questing heroine after all."

"Don't blame Helen," snapped Yann. "She would have gone back for it, but I didn't let her. I wanted her to heal Lavender and I heard the human police coming. So I wouldn't let her be a heroine. Not this time."

Helen took Lavender from Yann's gentle hands and used a very narrow bandage to secure the fairy's wing. She carefully folded the wing into its resting position, then moved the fairy's arm up and out of the way, so she could wind a figure of eight bandage round the wing, then round the torso. The bandage would hold the folded wing to the fairy's ribcage and stop it slipping out of the socket, or jerking around painfully. Not that Lavender would notice; she was still completely unconscious.

As she bandaged the fairy, Helen asked Lee, "Did you say those brownies were faeries?"

"Yes, our hairy domestic cousins. They prefer housework to parties. If they're given a little milk and bread, they'll work at night on the croft and in the house, doing the work the family don't have time to do. Sad creatures really."

"There were so many of them. Were they all from the castle?"

"No. They must have been from MacLeod households all over Skye."

"How did they know we were going to be there? We'd only just arrived. How could they have got to Dunvegan so fast, from all over the island?"

Lee didn't answer. He started to tidy up scattered first aid equipment.

She asked again, "How did they know we were coming to steal the flag, Lee?"

This time, when he didn't answer, Sylvie growled. Lee shrugged. "Perhaps the Queen warned them." He turned away, looking uncomfortable.

"Why would she do that?" Helen asked.

"Why not? If you succeed, she gets the flag. If not, she gets her music. Maybe she was trying to make the quest more interesting. More risky. A better tale for the bards."

Helen shook her head. "She set me a task to get a precious object for her, then warned those brownies I was coming so I was less likely to get it? That's a bit daft."

Lee handed her the wipes and bandages. "She's the Faery Queen. She isn't very predictable."

Yann sneered over their bent heads. "Tricksy folk, faeries. Not to be trusted *at all.*" He was looking at Lee.

"What were you doing, faery boy, while Lavender was being ripped limb from wing?"

"Fighting iron sickness, horse boy. What could I have done, anyway? Your fairy magic, centaur strength, human knowledge and wolf teeth didn't succeed. What could I have done? The whole point of your quest was that my people couldn't get the flag. But neither, it turns out, could your people."

Feeling the weight of her failure, Helen turned on Lee too. "You could have used your feathery hat to duel with the brownies' dusters. Or if you were too queasy to fight, you could at least have warned us your Queen was likely to undermine her own quest."

"She's not my Queen and I did warn you that the defences might not stop at the window."

"We were looking for human defences, not magical ones."

Yann said, "You bring nothing to this quest except a coward's fear of rust and the worry you're betraying us. Perhaps we should leave you here to make your own way home."

Lee stood up. "You didn't go into the castle with the girls either, hoofed one. So don't accuse me of cowardice." The two boys stared at each other. Lee put his hand on his sword. Yann scraped his hooves in the gritty white sand.

Sapphire rumbled. Yann nodded. "You're right. We may not trust him, but we're falling into a faery trap if we waste our time arguing with him." He looked at Helen. "We must decide what we do next."

Helen laid the silent fairy carefully in the top of the rucksack. "We fly back to the forest … and I admit my failure to the Queen."

Chapter 13

It was a quiet flight back over the sea from Skye.

Lavender was unconscious, wrapped in Helen's fleece in the top of the rucksack. Sylvie was silent, as Helen's tired arms held them both on the dragon's back. Yann was far behind them, galloping home. And Sapphire didn't often chat when she was flying.

Lee was the only one who wanted to talk. Whenever he tried to start a conversation, Helen ignored him, pretending the wind in her ears and the roar of Sapphire's wings prevented her from hearing him. Though as he was sitting right behind her and speaking in her ear, she could hear every word.

She didn't want his explanations, comfort or charm. She didn't want anything except a good night's sleep, then to get up tomorrow and play music. She wasn't a heroine after all. She was just a fiddler. She was a failure at adventures and quests.

Why hadn't she told Lavender to fly up above the brownies? She'd held the flag out of their reach, so why had she put Lavender on her shoulder, near their nasty hairy hands?

Why hadn't she thrown the box to Yann, rather than expecting him to reach for it?

Why had she held Lavender tighter than she had held the box? How could she have gripped her fragile friend so roughly?

Why hadn't she gone back in for the flag? Why had she let Yann hold her back? Her sudden shock at the police siren had been cowardly and irrational. The car had still been on the road, not at the door. She could have got into the castle and back out again with the flag before they arrived.

She was a failure. She had failed James, who was still in the hands of the faeries. She had failed the summer school students, who didn't even know they were in danger. She had failed the Faery Queen, who would probably not be polite about it.

She was a failure … and her pinky was still numb from the anaesthetic cream. She hoped she would be able to hold down the violin strings with it tomorrow. The idea of losing the soloist's spot because she'd anaesthetised her own hand made her snort with laughter. She used the sleeve of her fleece to wipe unexpected tears from her eyes.

Lee patted her on the shoulder. "The best adventures start with failure. You can still be a heroine, as well as a healer and a bard."

She yelled back, "I don't want to be a heroine. Or a healer. I'm far too young to make career choices."

"But you want to be a fiddler, don't you?"

"That's not a choice," she murmured. "That's just who I am."

They fell silent again, as Sapphire flew lower over the trees, landing in the total darkness of a cloudy Highland night near their clearing.

There was no point waiting for Yann. He would take hours to gallop back. But no one seemed in a hurry to set off for the Faery Queen's root cave. Lee started sharpening his sword. Sapphire lit a fire, as Helen carefully laid the snoring Lavender down, curled up on her right side, in a warm dry patch of leaves.

Sylvie barked at Helen.

Helen frowned at the wolf. Yann wasn't here. Lavender was still unconscious. How could she and Sylvie talk to each other?

Lee said, "Your wolf doesn't think you should humiliate yourself by admitting your failure to the Queen."

"You understand her wolf talk?"

"Of course." He laughed. "Just because we don't like each other, doesn't mean we don't understand each other. Sylvie thinks you should stay here by the fire, rather than admit to the Queen you didn't get the flag. What do you think, Helen?"

"I have to go. If I don't, I can't feed James, then he'll eat faery food and we'll never get him back."

Sylvie snorted.

Helen understood that comment without any help. "I know you don't think we'll ever get him back, but we have to leave the option open. We mustn't give up."

Helen rummaged in the rucksack, looking for a small bandage to use as a blanket for Lavender, so she could wear her fleece as protection against branches and thorns on the way to the Queen. Though a fleece was no protection against faery spears.

She laid a triangular bandage over the fairy, then bent down to take Lavender's tiny shoes off, so she didn't wake with sore feet as well as a sore shoulder.

She eased off the little indigo shoes, with their tiny white stiletto heels. Helen grimaced. Fairy fashion wasn't really her taste. Then she realized only the right shoe had a white heel; the left heel was dark purple. She looked closer at the right shoe. It wasn't the heel that was white: it was a corner of fabric, caught on the point of the stiletto. Pale cream fabric. Thin as a cobweb.

Lavender had been standing on the edge of the Fairy Flag when Helen jerked it out of the frame. Could this be …?

Helen looked at the three beings gazing sadly into the fire. She trusted Sapphire, but she didn't know Lee or Sylvie well enough to know whether they would let her take this to the Queen, or want it for themselves. So she put the scrap of silk in the tiny pocket hidden below the waistband of her jeans, then stood up.

"Jam sandwich delivery team to the ready."

Lee leapt up and put his sword back in his scabbard. Sylvie rose to her paws and shook her fur out.

Helen said, "Sylvie, could you please stay with Lavender? She mustn't get cold and stiffen up. Your paws will be better than Sapphire's claws at putting the bandage back if she throws it off. I'll go with Lee. He'll bring me back safe, won't you?"

Sylvie growled at him and Sapphire blew sparks on the fire until it blazed higher than the faery's head.

Lee laughed. "I'll promise to bring Helen back safely, if she promises not to accept another impossible quest!" Helen frowned, gesturing for him to lead on.

At first she wondered how they would find their way through the forest this late at night without moonlight, or starlight, or Lavender's light balls. She pulled the torch out of her pocket.

Then she realized she was having no problem seeing the forest floor between her and Lee, because his cloak was glowing in the darkness. She laughed and he said over his shoulder, "Glamour can be useful sometimes, even if you don't want me to charm you."

Helen walked behind him, wondering about his glamour and the spot she had seen just once, and whether it was wise to trust someone who didn't show you their true face.

"No one else trusts you, Lee. Can I really trust you?"

He didn't turn round. "We aren't a united band of adventurers like in the stories, Helen. We don't all want the same thing. Sylvie wants to drive my people out of the forest. Yann and Lavender have heard stories of our treachery all their lives. So perhaps they are right not to trust me.

"But you and I want the same thing. I'm charged by my King to prevent tension between humans on the forest edge and faeries at the centre. It's my duty to free the boy and to stop the Queen kidnapping your school of bards. So you can trust me, because we want the same thing."

"What if we don't want the same thing, some other day, Lee?"

He turned round. "Then some other day, you'll need to make that choice for yourself."

"So I should trust you, because I know what you want; but I shouldn't trust the Queen, because I don't know what she wants. Did she want the flag or not?"

Lee sighed in exasperation. "What does that woman want? Power, beauty, glory, treasure, parties, music, tricks, everyone at her feet? She doesn't know herself." He strode off through the trees.

"Let's find out if she really did want the flag or not." Helen patted her pocket and smiled.

As her fingers brushed the thin crease of fabric in her pocket, she thought about the Faery Queen's claim that the flag had power in every thread. She remembered old stories about magical spring water, strange ointment and fairy dust giving human eyes the power to see through glamour.

Was it worth a try?

She glanced at Lee, his red cloak shining like a warning light ahead of her. He was a charming friend. What would he be like as an enemy? Would he be offended if she tried to see through his glamour? But what use is a charming friend if you can't trust him?

It was worth a try.

She waited until they were crossing an open patch of ground, then called out, "Lee!" He whirled round.

Helen stuck her index finger in her pocket, scraped her nail across the fabric and poked her finger suddenly into her right eye.

Her eyelids slammed down in shock, but she blinked them open again, as her eye started to water.

Now she couldn't see Lee.

Of course not. His cloak was no longer glimmering. She switched her torch on.

There was a boy standing in front of her.

His blond hair was longer and messier, his skin was tanned and his cheekbones and jaw line were a little less Hollywood-perfect, but he still had a face that would make the older summer-school girls gossip and giggle. However, Lee's most charming feature, his smile, had vanished. He was frowning, looking stern and anxious.

Helen looked down.

She gulped back a burst of surprised laughter. This Lee, the true Lee, was wearing a grey t-shirt, a blue hooded sweatshirt, a pair of faded jeans and grubby white trainers. And his long shining sword.

She looked at his face again.

He was smiling now. A cheerful open grin, showing white teeth overlapping slightly at the front. But he had no spots at all. He raised his eyebrows. "Seen enough?"

Helen felt suddenly embarrassed at staring so hard. She blinked. She must have blinked the last of the flag's power out of her eye, because when she looked again, Lee was dressed in a cloak, with pale skin and perfect teeth.

She looked away. "Sorry," she muttered. "I just needed to know."

"Know what?"

"Who you are."

"You know better now, do you? Does what I wear, or what I look like when I haven't brushed my hair, tell you any more about who I am?"

She shook her head, ashamed.

"Do you trust me more or less now?"

"I think I trusted you anyway. I was just curious. That was unfair. I'm sorry."

She stepped round him and kept walking towards the root caves. They didn't speak for five minutes.

When Helen reached a clump of trees she didn't recognise, she waited for Lee to lead the way again. She said quietly as he brushed past, "I know it was rude to try to see what you're really like, like peeking at someone in the changing rooms to see their underwear or something. But I have to ask. Jeans? And trainers?"

"Yeah. So what?"

"It's not exactly traditional, is it?"

"You're hardly wearing fair maiden clothes yourself. I don't have to dress in clothes from hundreds of years ago any more than you do. These clothes are comfy, practical and very useful for quests."

Helen grinned. "Were you wearing jeans last week, Lee, or did you only get them once you met me? Are you copying me?"

Now Lee looked embarrassed. "I wasn't on a quest last week, Helen."

"If you're wearing jeans and a t-shirt, why are you glamouring a cloak and boots and feathery hat. Why not just show the real you?"

"They're both the real me. I like the cloak. It's good for swirling and for impressing people. And it makes me look exactly like a faery is expected to look, so hulking macho idiots like your centaur underestimate me. He thinks he knows exactly who I am: a fop and a fool. He doesn't take me seriously because he only sees the silk and the velvet."

"Do you enjoy being treated like that?"

"Not really, but it can be useful. So can the light from my cloak, can't it?"

"You don't have any spots, do you?" Helen asked, as they crossed the grove of tall straight pines.

"No. Never."

"Then why do you glamour a spot beside your nose?"

"What did you think when you saw the spot? When we first met?"

"I thought your glamour wasn't working on me. I thought I could see through you, to your flaws."

"Did it make you trust me more?"

"It made me less afraid of you. More confident I could deal with you."

Lee nodded. "Good. Worth a little blemish then."

Helen laughed. "It's all about appearances for you! You wouldn't have to make people underestimate you or be less afraid of you if you were just yourself!"

Lee looked at her seriously. "Don't assume that just because you've seen me in a pair of jeans you know who I am, or what I can do." He straightened his sword on his hip and marched off.

Helen paused for a moment, then followed him to the edge of the clearing. She was about to move past him, when he held out his arm in front of her chest. "I have just one question for you, human girl. How did you do that? How did you see through me so easily?"

She smiled. "Watch and you'll find out." She ducked under his arm, stabbing her torch beam into the dark clearing.

His voice called softly after her, "Please don't try any tricks with the Queen, Helen. She won't be as tolerant as I am."

The torch light only showed Helen tiny patches of the clearing, so it was hard to get her bearings, and she blundered about looking for the right root cave.

She felt the empty space on her shoulder, where Lavender usually stood, chattering and advising. Even though she hadn't listened to the fairy's advice last night, she missed her. She felt very alone.

But she wasn't alone. Suddenly, she could see the boy in a pit at her feet.

"James!" Helen pushed through the thick air.

He looked up, with pale cheeks and dark eyes.

"James! I've brought you a picnic!"

She swung the rucksack round, pulling out the sandwiches.

"Catch!" She threw the packet straight at him. "Jam with no crusts and no butter. They're your favourites, aren't they?"

She couldn't get him to smile. He just looked up dully, then glanced away again.

She threw the bottle of water through the space between them. "Don't eat anything else until I come back, James. I'm going to take you home..."

He was already fading. He clutched the water and the sandwiches to his chest, before vanishing into the back wall of the cave.

Helen didn't look behind her. She didn't want to know if she was surrounded by spears. So she watched as the Queen walked in smooth elegant steps towards her. Helen could see she was on the back wall all the time, getting bigger and brighter with every step, but no closer. Maybe she was walking on a path somewhere else entirely.

Now the Queen was as tall as Helen. Taller. As tall as Yann. She stopped, though the billowing waves of her sea-coloured dress kept moving around her. The fabric glowed so brightly that Helen switched her torch off.

"Do you bring me the flag?"

"Do you really want it?"

"Of course I want it! Why else would I agree to swap my darling little human boy, Johnny, or whatever his name is, and my precious midsummer musicians for it?"

"You said one thread of the flag was worth all ten of my fingers. Is that true?"

"Oh yes. Anything of faery making is worth far more than any human skill, or any human life."

"Then the twenty people at the summer school and the one boy you've stolen are worth less than twenty-one threads of that flag?"

The Queen shrugged. "If you want to get arithmetical about it, I suppose so. But I want the whole flag."

"I've brought you more than twenty-one threads. I've brought you this." Helen took out the scrap of flag.

The Queen looked at it in horror. "You *tore* it?"

"It got ripped. We were attacked."

"Attacked? By brownies? They don't attack, they just tidy up."

"They tidied one of my friends so much she was a different shape afterwards. The flag got ripped, but I've brought you this. Worth more than my fingers, more than the summer school, more than the boy. So let him go and free me from my obligation to provide you with music. Then I'll give you this."

"Swap the boy and the music for a tiny bit of silk? Never. You have failed. I will keep the boy now until you have played for me."

"No!"

"Yes. That corner of flag is not worth anything on its own. It's not the flag we want. It's the promise. We need to be free of the promise to provide warriors at the whim of a human. You have left the MacLeods with the flag, so they can wave it whenever they choose. That threat still hangs over us. So you still owe me music."

Helen glanced over her shoulder. She *was* surrounded by faery warriors, with scowls and spears. She was trapped until she reached an agreement with the Queen.

She sighed and looked back at the Queen. "You want to be freed from the promise?"

"Yes."

"Then you'll give me the boy and I won't have to provide midsummer music?"

The Queen frowned at Helen, then smiled. "You can't free us from the promise, you don't have the flag."

"Yes, I can," said Helen triumphantly. "I can free you right now."

She held the scrap of silk up between her thumb and forefinger. She waved it in the night air. It started to disintegrate, tiny threads floating off to vanish in the dark. She waved it, once, twice, three times, over her head.

The Queen's perfect oval face turned white.

There was an explosion of noise at the other side of the clearing. Hooves slammed against the earth, hurtling out of the night towards Helen.

The dozen spearmen of the Queen's guard leapt past Helen and stood in the root cave, their spears pointing up at the attacking cavalry, guarding their Queen, or perhaps the path to her.

Helen stood still. Breath caught in her chest, her hand trembling above her head.

Horses crashed to a halt behind and around her. She could hardly see them, just their shapes in the darkness, barely lit by the Queen's faded pastel glow. But she could smell them, their salty sweat and their cold breath, and she could hear them, jingling and snorting.

The men on the horses had spears too. Three long blades thrust past Helen to land shivering at the rim of the hollow.

She was surrounded by soldiers. By weapons, fear and anger. She stood very still, wondering what she had summoned with a few fragile threads of silk.

She seemed to have called up a war.

Chapter 14

A voice boomed out of the darkness. "Who has summoned us?"

Helen swallowed her doubts, then said clearly, "I have."

"Where is your enemy?"

Helen pointed at the Queen.

The Queen took a step backwards, which didn't take her any further away; she was already on the back wall of the cave. Then she remembered she was somewhere else entirely and stood up straight again.

The deep voice laughed. "What have you done, my Queen? How did you give this much power to so small a child?"

There was a clattering thump, as someone dismounted behind Helen, then strode to the edge of the root cave.

He stood between the quivering spears, a tall man in black armour and a radiant golden cloak.

Helen said quickly, "I don't want you to attack her, I just want to get the boy back."

"A boy, my Queen?" He sighed. "Not again!"

"It's a bargain between me and the girl, my King. None of your concern. She has said she does not want you to attack me, so she has released you from your Fairy Flag promise. You may go."

"I would like to stay and see what bargain you've made with this intriguing human child."

"None that has yet been fulfilled."

"Yes it has," Helen insisted. "You wanted the power of the promise broken, so I waved the flag a third time and the MacLeods can never again summon a faery army. Now you must give me back the boy and find your own entertainment for the revels."

"No, that was not the bargain," the Queen said. "The boy was to be exchanged for the flag, but you have destroyed the tiny bit of flag you managed to retrieve."

Helen looked at her fingertips. Just one pale length of thread stuck to her thumb, so she pushed it back in her pocket. "But I used up the promise. That was what you wanted."

"It may have been what I *wanted*, but it was not what we *agreed*. Yesterday we agreed the flag for the boy. Today I told you why I wanted it. You kindly removed the promise for me, but that wasn't our original agreement. Our original agreement was the flag for the boy. You haven't brought me a flag, so I keep the boy until you play for me at midsummer."

"But I said I would release you from the promise in return for the boy!" Helen yelled in frustration.

"So you did. However, I did not agree to that bargain. I just doubted you could do it, then you took up the challenge. But you didn't get an agreement from me first, did you?"

"That isn't fair!"

"Yes it is. I intended to display the flag at my party, but now I have nothing to show. Instead I'll let my guests hear the best young musicians in the land. Then you will get the boy."

"No. I need the boy now," Helen appealed to the King, "because soon his family will know he's gone. Then they'll come and hunt the forests for him."

The King looked at her. He had a neat black beard and deep brown eyes. He was as handsome as his Queen was beautiful, and as bright as Lee was glowing, but it wasn't a layer of shining light. It was a fire inside. This faery wasn't bending light. He was creating it.

He shook his head. "I cannot interfere in a bargain between a faery and a human."

He walked back to his horse, leaning forward as he passed Helen and whispering, "Finish this quest, human child, the way you've begun it, and all will end happily ever after."

As the King climbed on his horse, the Queen laughed, her dress bright and swirling again. The spear faeries relaxed as the horses galloped away.

Helen clenched her fists, nails digging into her palms. She had failed. Failed to use the scrap of flag to get an agreement from the Queen, failed to use the army she had called up to save herself or James.

The Queen spoke sharply to Helen. "Off you go then. Go and rehearse, instead of wasting your time on quests you can't handle. You need to be at your best for midsummer night."

"At my best, for you? You must be joking. You're a liar and a cheat!"

The Queen raised her eyebrows in gently offended surprise.

"You sent me on a quest, which I undertook in good faith, but you broke that faith by warning the brownies we were coming to steal the flag."

"Oh no, I ..."

"Oh yes, you did. How else did you know what had attacked us, before I told you?"

Helen pointed her finger at the Queen. "You made a bargain to give me James if I brought you a treasure, which you then set a guard over. Then I gave you what you really wanted, released you from that inconvenient promise, but you're still not giving me anything in return.

"You are a cheat and a trickster and have no honour at all!"

The Queen laughed. "All that may be true. But I still have the boy ... and you have nothing to bargain with, except your ability to play music!

"If you and your friends play for my revels, I will let the boy go. If you don't, I will keep him forever. That was our bargain."

"No, the bargain was that I would provide music, not that I would play music. There's a difference. If you give me the boy, I will *provide* you with music."

The Queen shook her head in disappointment. "Did

you think I hadn't noticed that little play on words? Did you think you could weasel out that way? You can't trick the tricksters, girl!

"I don't want your recordings or downloadings. They aren't real music. They are just the ghosts of live music. I want living breathing musicians. Only for that will I give you back the boy."

Helen grew cold in the dark. Her clever wording hadn't been clever enough.

The Queen smiled at Helen. "I leave it up to your conscience how you get those musicians. If you choose to bring your summer school friends unknowing to my door, then run away and save yourself, I will understand.

"Though I would love," her voice sank to a purr, "I would love to hear *you* play. Perhaps the honourable thing would be to take full responsibility yourself alone. Then you would have no guilt, just a warm sense of sacrifice, to keep you company all the years you serve me.

"Your choice. Yourself. Or your friends. But I will have my music. Or the boy stays here."

Helen took a deep breath. "This living breathing music. Where must I bring it? And when?"

The Queen smiled graciously. "You will be very welcome at the green hill in the west of Dorry Shee forest two nights from now. The revels start at midnight. Please arrive in plenty of time to tune up."

She swept away, unpinning her long pale hair as she went.

Helen kicked at the edge of the hollow, watching with satisfaction as a lump of earth fell off.

She looked at the line of spear-faeries in the pit below

her. "Sorry about summoning an army against you. No hard feelings?"

They stared at her. Still pointing their blades at her. She shrugged, turned her back on them and walked slowly and calmly to the trees, because she couldn't run faster than a thrown spear anyway.

As she reached the edge of the clearing, Lee appeared, bursting with anxious questions.

"What did you *do* out there? Did you really summon a faery army? What were you *thinking?* Was that a fragment of the flag you had? Where did you get it? Was that how you managed to see me earlier?"

Helen answered the simplest question. "I got the fragment of flag from Lavender's shoe. Her heel ripped it off when we were attacked."

"But why did you wave it without getting an absolutely solid agreement from the Queen?"

"That was my big mistake. I wasn't listening hard enough."

"You have to weigh every word she speaks. She twists words even more easily than light. If you didn't get a new bargain from her, how will you free the boy?"

Helen sighed. "I have a decision to make. Either I play music for her myself, or I provide her with some other poor fools. Or else James stays there for ever."

"Helen…"

"It's my decision. Let me think."

They walked through the trees, silently. Neither of them saw a tall boy with shaggy black hair leaning casually against an ancient pine. He ran his long-nailed fingers through his hair and slid round the tree to keep them in sight.

Helen struggled to keep up with Lee. Her thoughts kept slowing her down. She'd thought she was so clever, saying she would *provide* rather than play music. But the Queen had twisted so many bargains and she was impossible to fool.

Helen had no decision to make, not really. She couldn't leave James with the Faery Queen. And she couldn't give the Queen anyone else. Not even Zoe. She would have to play herself.

When they arrived at the clearing, Helen sat down and tried to stop her hands trembling by warming them at the campfire. She only half listened to Lee telling Sylvie and Sapphire about the Faery Queen's demands and Helen's decision.

Helen noticed that Sylvie and Sapphire were actually listening to the faery, rather than being rude. Helen smiled. Perhaps they could be friends after all. She couldn't though. She wouldn't be here.

She had to leave. Now. Before she started to cry.

She stood up. "I have to go. I have to rehearse."

Sapphire growled. Lee said, "Don't give up yet. We still have one night. We can do a lot in one night."

Helen laughed bitterly. "Yes. We have one night. Only one night. Because we've spent a couple of nights on this stupid quest. She used the flag quest to distract us, to make us waste time.

"I'm not wasting any more sleeping or rehearsal time on impossible and pointless quests. I'm going back to the lodge."

Helen looked at Sylvie, sitting sadly by the fire. "Have you called your brothers off, or will I be followed by wolves again tonight?"

Sylvie put her head on her paws and whined a brief answer to Lee.

"She gives you her word there are no wolves watching you tonight." He smiled. "I think we should walk you home anyway, otherwise you might fall asleep on the path."

Sylvie and Lee walked beside Helen as she trudged towards the lodge in the headachey light of dawn.

As they neared the back of the lodge, she looked at the faery and the wolf. "I'm sorry I'm letting you both down. I'm sorry I haven't prevented the Queen's party. I will try to think of a way out of this for all of us, but I need to sleep first."

Before they could answer, Helen turned away and plodded towards her bedroom.

Chapter 15

Helen tugged off her filthy boots and looked at the clock. It was nearly 5 am.

Everyone else in the lodge must have been asleep for hours. She shrugged. They'd had enough sleep already.

So she hauled out her fiddle and started to play Professor Greenhill's masterpiece.

She played wildly, fumbling notes with her numb pinkie. At first she put all her dark forest terrors into the music, then she noticed lighter tones sneak in and recognised the guilty excitement she felt at the idea of performing for the Faery Queen and her court.

Suddenly, she thought of her little sister. If she performed for the Queen, James would play with Emma this weekend, but Helen might never see Nicola again.

She stood at the window, playing more slowly.

She saw a curtain twitch over in the old lodge. Was that the Professor's window? The curtains opened and Fay Greenhill looked out. She was brushing her silver hair, winding it up into that messy bun. She waved at Helen. Helen played faster again, more cheerfully now. It was always easier with an audience.

Helen played herself calm and lay down on her bed at last. The gaps in her morning timetable meant she could sleep for a few hours.

However, when she woke up, long after breakfast-time, she didn't feel rested at all.

She could hear pipes and flutes from the barn. She checked the clock. 10 am. Time for a slice of toast before her late morning lesson with the Professor.

She had hoped to find someone in the kitchen after her shower, because a chat about music would have been better than thinking about her failures and her fate.

Zoe was not the person she had been hoping for.

The older violinist was gazing into a steaming mug of coffee and didn't even notice Helen making sandwiches as well as toast. After five minutes of silence, Zoe blurted out, "Have you heard about the solo yet?"

"No," answered Helen, tapping her left pinkie against the table to see if it was still numb.

"I can't stand not knowing. How can you be so calm about it? Are you too young and stupid to understand how important it is?"

Helen winced as her pinkie throbbed. "I do know how important this midsummer music is, but I have other things to worry about."

She picked up the sandwiches, taking them to her room before going to the old lodge for her last lesson with the Professor. She tried to feel enthusiastic as she walked past the piles of leaflets in the untidy corridor.

She knocked and the Professor's cheerful voice summoned her into the study. "My early morning muse! You played beautifully this morning. What a lovely way to be woken up. But my dear, you look a little worried.

"Come and play me the music that inspires you. Come and lose yourself in the music."

That sounded like a very good idea. Helen played the tune she and her friend Rona had written last year. She couldn't help smiling as her music filled the study, remembering the successful quests it described.

Losing herself in music did work. Perhaps that was how she needed to look at her decision to play for the Faery Queen. She would spend the rest of her life lost in music.

She put the bow and violin down gently and shook her hands out.

The Professor smiled at Helen through her waving silver hair and adjusted her bright scarf. "I'm sorry I've kept you all waiting for my decision about the solo. I hope it hasn't distracted you from your other concerns?"

Helen shook her head politely, if not entirely honestly.

"Well, my dear, you're the most promising young fiddler I've heard in years, so I've no hesitation in offering you the violin solo tomorrow night. But ..." the Professor's voice cut sharper than usual, "... but there is a condition."

Helen, who had made a mess of too many bargains over the last few days, raised her eyebrows in surprise.

"You're a night owl and an early bird. I keep an eye on my students and I've seen you wandering about. This gives us an opportunity.

"Performing in the middle of the night is a very different skill from performing during the day, or in the evening. Bringing the night alive. Making the blackness breathe. Using the power of the dark to make the music stronger. Those are the skills I need from you at midsummer.

"So I will give you the soloist's spot, but only if you will have a midnight lesson with me tonight."

Helen frowned.

"Stay here with me tonight. Play for me at midnight, play for me until the sun rises. Then you will be my soloist for this concert and, I'm sure, for many others.

"If you do not give me that commitment," she flicked her hair over her shoulder, "then I will give the solo to someone else."

Helen patted the pocket of her clean jeans. She wished she was still wearing her manky jeans, with the fragment of the Fairy Flag in her pocket. She wished she still had the power to see through glamour.

Then she realized she didn't need the thread to give her that power.

She could see clearly what she was being offered, without any magic at all.

Helen was being offered what she wanted most of all, but to get it she had to sacrifice her chance of finding a way to save both James and herself.

She looked closely at the Professor. Who was she? What was she?

That didn't really matter. What mattered was what she was trying to do. The Professor was trying to keep Helen here all night, rather than in the forest with her friends, for the same reason that the Faery Queen had sent her to Skye. So she couldn't search for an alternative to playing tomorrow night.

Helen smiled. The Professor looked relieved.

But Helen had smiled because now she had hope. If queens and professors were trying to stop her finding an answer, that must mean there was an answer out there.

She smiled wider and opened her lips to say "no." Her voice caught in her throat. It was was hard, really hard, to turn down a solo spot that she wanted so much.

The Professor was staring at her. "Come on, Helen. Is the decision so difficult to make?"

"No, it's not difficult. Thanks for the offer ... but I can't accept it."

The Professor frowned. "I hope you don't regret that decision."

Helen packed away her fiddle and bow, then opened the door. "I won't regret it. Thanks for all I've learnt, Professor."

She left the study, went back to bed and slept a calm restful sleep, at last sure of what she needed to do that night.

She woke up just in time for the school's first rehearsal with the soloists. In the barn, with the stuffed animals set up in a row like an audience, Professor Greenhill ignored Helen and fussed over her soloists. Stewart on cello, Catriona on pipes, Juliet's friend Amelia on flute, Tommy on bodhran drum and, of course, Zoe on fiddle, fizzing with excitement.

Helen stood at the back of the violin section trying to ignore the wolf staring at her with glassy eyes. After a good afternoon's sleep, she was wondering if she'd overreacted this morning. Surely Professor Greenhill wasn't conspiring with the Faery Queen? She was a well-known academic. Surely the offer of a night-time lesson had been a genuine attempt to help Helen adapt to different ways of playing.

What a daft thing to do ... throwing away the chance of a solo!

Helen gritted her teeth as she watched Zoe put rosin on her bow with a flourish and pride that should have been Helen's.

Then she saw the Professor's narrow pink heels teeter about the dust and rubble of the barn, never picking up any dirt, and reminded herself that she would have the rest of her life to play solos, but only if she found a way round the Faery Queen's demands tonight. The Professor's solo and Helen's desire to play it were distractions, just like the quest for the flag.

That evening, for the first time, the Professor conducted the whole orchestra. When Zoe began the violin solo, the Professor stood high on her pointy toes, peering into the back of the barn, to look straight at Helen. Her tight smile was not pleasant at all.

Helen was scribbling: In a bad mood. Leave me alone, by her name on the clipboard, when Alice came down the stairs and glanced at the form.

"Are you upset about the solo? Going for another early night?"

Helen grunted.

"Don't worry. No one will come hunting for you. Every player understands disappointment."

Helen grinned as Alice turned away, then stomped loudly up the stairs, tiptoed back down and crept out of the side door.

She rushed breathless into the clearing ten minutes later, gasping, "The Faery Queen isn't hijacking the summer school!"

Helen glanced round, looking for Lavender. She was awake, perched on Yann's shoulder, her bandage still pristine white. Helen reached out for the fairy and Yann passed her down.

Helen explained as she unwound Lavender's bandage. "The Professor has been organizing this concert *for* the midsummer revels!"

Sylvie, who was sitting on the lowest branch of the beech tree, dressed in her grey fleece again, with no bandage on her arm, said sarcastically. "Obviously! Didn't you realize that? Why else would the best young musicians in Scotland be here, now, playing that magical music?"

Helen frowned up at Sylvie. "When did you work that out? Why didn't you tell me?"

Yann laughed. "We worked it out about five minutes ago. Your Professor is either enchanted or in league with the Faery Queen."

Helen nodded. "The Professor tried to keep me there this evening with the promise of a solo part … but I turned it down. Can you flap your wing, Lavender?"

"You turned down a faery bargain that would have fed your ambition?" asked Lavender. "Good for you." She winced as she stretched her wing.

"So I realized that if everyone is trying to stop us

doing something this evening, there must be something we can do."

"No," said Sylvie. "This has gone on long enough. This is no longer a quest, nor an adventure. This is now a war. I will not let you go over to the enemy, human child, because you have healed me, and I don't want to fight you. So I cannot let you play for her tomorrow."

"That's okay. I'm not going to play for her tomorrow. I'm going to find someone else to play."

"No! If you find some other living breathing musicians for her, then she'll still have her party and she'll still be invading my forest. All you musicians must leave Dorry Shee before midsummer night, then her party will flop and she'll leave."

"But then she'll take James with her!" Helen yelled in frustration. She passed the fairy back up to Yann, so Lavender could exercise her wing without being shouted over.

Sylvie shook her head. "You've done well to keep the boy human for such a long time, but he was lost the moment they laid hands on him. He may have forgotten his family by now."

"He remembers jam sandwiches. And his family haven't forgotten him."

"You cannot save him, because I will not let these revels go ahead."

"You? On your own?"

"No. Me, my brothers, my pack…"

"Sylvie, this boy is someone's brother too." Helen tried to speak more calmly. "I promise if you will help me tonight, then once James is free, I'll help you drive the faeries from the forest."

Sylvie looked down her long nose at Helen. "What use is that promise? What use is your help? Everything you have touched so far has failed."

"So you don't need to worry about me succeeding tonight then, do you?" Helen's voice rose. "If everything I do fails, then I might fail tonight too. But I'm not going to give up until I've tried. Will you help me?"

Sylvie jumped to the ground, landing softly on all fours. "I will listen … then decide."

Yann said, "We will all help. First, tell us exactly what the Faery Queen said to you last night. I would rather hear it from you than from him," he gestured at Lee, standing at the edge of the clearing.

So Helen, Lee, Yann and Lavender crowded round the fire, Sapphire shuffled to sit nearby without squashing anyone, and Sylvie sat sceptically further away. Helen wound the bandage gently round Lavender's wing again, and explained, "The Faery Queen wants a living breathing musician. It doesn't have to be me. I can betray someone else to her and still get the boy; she would be amused by that. But I won't buy the boy's safety at the cost of anyone else's. Except mine, of course."

"And we will not let you do that," Yann insisted. "There must be an alternative."

"I had planned to give her a recording and even the equipment to play it on, but the words 'living breathing' cancel out all the alternatives I had come up with. She will accept nothing but a real live musician."

"Does it have to be human?"

"You mean like a selkie singing? I couldn't do that to another fabled beast. They would be trapped with that awful woman forever."

Yann scraped his hoof at the edge of the fire. "So you will only give her another musician if you can be sure you're not putting that musician in danger?"

"Yes, so we're looking for a musician talented enough to play for them and strong enough to walk out of their mound; someone used to the ways of faeries.

"You keep calling me your bard, which I'm not. I'm just a fiddler. But there have been real bards, haven't there? Have any bards played for the faeries and escaped from them before? If we can find someone like that, we've found our alternative."

Lavender nodded enthusiastically, much happier now her wing was supported again. "Do you have someone in mind?"

Helen shook her head. "I don't know any bards. I thought you might."

So Yann, Lavender and Lee started to name drop.

"Orpheus?"

"No, he'd just put us all to sleep."

"Pan?"

"Not another stinky faun!"

"Thomas the Rhymer?"

"No, he went back to the faeries in the end. He might even be there tomorrow."

"The Viking skald, Nornagest?"

"No, ever since the scare with the candle, he doesn't like performing at night."

Sapphire growled a suggestion, which made Sylvie laugh cynically.

Then they had run out of ideas. Helen wondered if she was going to have to play her fiddle tomorrow after all. She pictured her fiddle, an old instrument in a modern case, and remembered the story her grandfather had told about it.

"What about Ossian? One of his descendants made my fiddle ... or so my grandpa says. Ossian was a bard in stories, wasn't he? Is he real?"

Lee leapt up, his cloak bright with excitement. "Ossian! Brilliant idea! He is a true Celtic hero and bard. His poetry and music were so wonderful that Scottish songbirds still sing his songs. And he escaped from my people once before, from a mound in Speyside. He escaped unharmed with his harp still in his hand. He'd be perfect if we could find him!"

Helen sighed, realizing her own idea was no better than the others. "It will be impossible to find any of them! I was hoping for more modern bards. Someone playing in Glasgow or Manchester or Ibiza. All these names are from myths and legends. All these bards must be dead by now. Even Ossian must have played his harp hundreds of years ago."

Lee nodded. "He played his first song, to warn his mother that his father's hounds were hunting her, more than a thousand years ago."

"If he's been dead for centuries, he can't help us tomorrow night."

"He might not be dead," said Lee. "The Celtic heroes were always offered the chance of eternal youth, so if Ossian chose to pay the price, he'll be with the rest of the Fianna in Tir nan Og."

"Tir nan Og?" Helen stumbled over the name.

Yann laughed. "Now that truly is a mythical place."

"Where is it?" Helen asked. "What price do you pay?"

"In stories it's the land of the ever young, found

westwards over the sea, straight into the setting sun. It's not real," said Yann.

Lee disagreed. "It is real and he might be there."

"What's the price?" Helen asked again.

Lee answered. "The price of dwelling in Tir nan Og, where the apple trees bear both blossom and fruit all year, is your memory. You stay forever young, but you can't remember your life on this land."

"He'll not be much use to us if he can't remember how to play his harp!"

"No, it's just the memory of self that goes. The fingers will remember their skills. The warriors still fight, the bards still play. He may not remember the names of the tunes he plays, nor where he learnt them, but he will still play like the famous poet and bard that he is."

"Then let's go west and find him." Helen stood up.

No one else did.

"Come on!" she urged, starting to cover the fire with cold earth.

"But how do we get there?" objected Yann. "We only have one night."

"Yes," said Helen, "so we need to hurry, because the sun is setting. And we have to fly straight towards it. Come on!"

This time, everyone got up.

Chapter 16

"Where are we going, Helen?" Yann demanded.

"Tir nan Og."

"But where is it?" he shouted after Helen as she ran to the forest edge.

"I don't know, but if the Queen doesn't want us to go, it must be possible to get there. So let's find it."

They all squashed onto the dragon's back. Even Yann. "I'm not letting you lot go without me this time. Not when it's always such a disaster."

He kicked Sapphire's wing joint with a back hoof as he clambered on. She growled a query.

"How long am I going to be up here?" Yann muttered. "How should I know? How far is it to somewhere that doesn't exist? As far as we're prepared to go before we turn back."

"We're not turning back," said Helen. "This is one quest that's going to succeed."

Sapphire took off, so slow and low Helen was worried the dragon couldn't fly with Yann's weight. But as soon as Sapphire was out of sight of the lodge, she stopped scraping her scales along the top of the dark trees, swooped fast up into the air and headed west, towards the setting sun.

"Where are we going?" Yann yelled again.

Helen unfolded the tourist map of Skye and the other Hebrides, the edges flapping in the wind. "Which island is it? Will it be on the map?"

"Possibly," Lee yelled back. "It won't be called Tir nan Og though. Some stories say Rockall is the Land of the Ever Young. Can you find that on your chart?"

Sapphire grunted and Sylvie laughed. "Sapphire's flown races to Rockall and back. It's just a tiny rock out in the Atlantic. It's not a magical retirement home for heroes."

Lee tried again. "What about Holm or Fladda-chuain off Skye? Both of them are mentioned in Tir nan Og stories."

Helen stared at the map, impaling the Western Isles on a silver spike to try to hold it steady. She shook her head.

"Holm is just a few hundred metres off the coast. Far too close to people and roads. Fladda's a bit further out. Shall we try it first? Sapphire, please fly to Skye again, then find the northern tip of the main island!"

As Sapphire flew high above the mountains, Helen saw glens and lochs laid out below them, long deep lines scratched into Scotland like claw marks.

Sapphire had accelerated as soon as she had a destination, so Helen had to yell even louder. "We know where we're going now, but what do we know about Ossian? How can we persuade him to help us?"

Lee yelled back, "He's one of the Fianna, the ancient warrior band of Finn McCool. They defended the kings of Scotland and Ireland thousands of years ago."

Helen frowned. "I thought he was a musician, not a warrior."

"To join the Fianna you had to defend yourself against nine spears with just a stick and a shield, but you also had to compose a song, memorise twelve books of poetry, sprint while taking a thorn from your foot, jump the height of your head, run through a wood without letting one hair be caught on a twig, and after being chased by all the Fianna and escaping unmarked, you had to hold your weapon without it trembling in your hand. Ossian could do all that, but he was the best of them at song."

Now Sapphire was flying over the sea, over a narrow stretch of water tied down by the thin Skye bridge. Then she turned to her right, gently and slowly, so as not to dislodge Yann.

Helen asked, "Will the Fianna be the only people on Tir nan Og?"

Yann snorted. "We'll never know. We're never going to find Tir nan Og in the first place …"

Lavender murmured a more helpful answer in her ear. "There might be other, earlier, Celtic heroes there. Even more violent ones than the Fianna." Helen felt the fairy tremble. "Look to your left. Do you see those spiky mountains?"

"Those are the Cuillins," shouted Helen, glad to be able to answer a question rather than ask them all.

"The Cuillins are named after Cuchullin," said Lavender. "A Celtic warrior who once fought for six whole days and nights in those mountains. I hope he won't be there."

Helen shook her head. "How on earth are we going to persuade these ancient heroes to help us?"

Sylvie growled, "Shouldn't you have thought of that before we took off?"

Helen shrugged. "Let's start by asking nicely. I'm sure a real hero will be delighted to rescue a wee boy from an evil queen."

The Cuillins had vanished behind them into the fading light and they were now over the very north of Skye. Just a few miles out to sea, they found Fladda-chuain. The long thin island didn't look at all magical, not even in the late evening sun.

Sapphire flew up the low spine of the island and back again. They saw a ruined chapel, but no other buildings. They saw a few scurrying black rabbits and some coarse grass, but no people and no apple trees.

"It's not here," grumbled Yann, trying to keep his balance as Sapphire swerved over the dark basalt at the north-west tip of the island.

"Obviously, it's not here if you just arrive by sea or wings, otherwise anyone could find it," said Lee. "But it might be possible to get to it from here."

"How?" asked Helen.

"I don't know. We faeries get our own kind of immortality. We don't have to buy it with our memories. So I don't know."

Helen watched the sun settle onto the horizon. "We don't have much time!" she yelled. "Any ideas?"

"Puffins!" Lavender pointed to a flock of puffins, their tiny wings flapping frantically as they flew along the rocky shore.

"I love watching puffins too," Helen said impatiently, "but we need to concentrate on getting to Tir nan Og."

"Watch the puffins," insisted Lavender. "All Scotland's birds originally came from Tir nan Og. Perhaps those puffins are going back."

Sapphire hovered so her passengers could watch the dozen puffins fly sunwise round the island. As they reached the south-eastern corner for the second time, the birds vanished. The air their wings had been beating was suddenly empty.

"Fly sunwise," shouted Helen. "Fly clockwise round the island. Fly round twice."

Sapphire flew round twice, and as they reached the skerries of the south-eastern tip for the second time, Helen gripped the spike in front of her in expectation. Nothing happened. They were still flying round an empty grassy island. Sapphire slowed down.

"Don't slow down," yelled Yann. "Keep going. Lavender, were the puffins already flying when you spotted them?"

"Yes."

"Then keep going round, Sapphire. As many times as you have the energy for."

As the dragon rounded the south-eastern corner for the third time, turning to fly straight into the rays of the setting sun, she flinched from the light, misjudged the tight turn and dipped her wings sharply.

Yann, whose horse body wasn't secure on the dragon's back even when she was flying upright, started to slide off towards the dark rocks below.

Helen grabbed for his arm, Lee reached for his tail, but they both missed.

Yann fell off the speeding dragon. Helen closed her eyes and felt Sapphire dive after him.

Splash!

The spray of fresh water drops surprised Helen into opening her eyes.

Sapphire was clambering out of a shallow river onto the soft grass of its bank, where Yann was leaping uninjured to his hooves. Helen, Sylvie and Lee slid off.

They had been above the Minch a moment ago, but now there was no grey seawater to be seen.

Nor was the sun setting in the west. It was overhead, warming a bright afternoon.

Flowers were blooming by the water, daffodils and roses at the same time. Helen saw brambles, blossoming white and ripening purple on the same branch.

The friends stood together, backs to the shallow water, facing a wave of people moving slowly towards them.

All young, beautiful, glowing with health and happiness. Walking arm in arm, or in gently strolling groups. Looking with a complete lack of curiosity at the children who had fallen into their river.

When the first half dozen of them stopped nearby, Helen spoke politely. "We're looking for Ossian."

Lee shushed her and declaimed in a herald's voice: "We seek the bard Ossian, to pay homage to his mastery of song and to ask a favour of one famed for his heroism and his compassion for those in need."

"Okay," nodded Helen. "We're doing that too."

"Welcome to our land," said a woman in a cream dress. "Come with us, if you wish."

The group of men and women wandered off along the river, as if they'd all the time in the world. Helen kept striding ahead and overtaking them. Yann grabbed her shoulder. "Don't be so impatient."

Soon they came to a gathering of men. Taller, stronger, hardier than the people strolling by the river. Dressed in leathers and checks, yellow and red cloaks held by large round pins at their shoulders. Sitting in a circle, chatting and laughing, petting huge hairy hounds, sharpening swords and spear heads.

"The Fianna," said Lavender in Helen's ear. "The warrior band of Finn McCool. All choosing to pay the price of eternal youth."

Lee stepped forward and spoke:

"To the son of Finn McCool, we pay respect for your gift of music,

"To the father of Osgar, we pay respect for your prowess in battle,

"To the brother of Fergus, we pay respect for your skill in the hunt,

"To the friend of St Patrick, we pay respect …"

As Lee's list got longer and more elaborate, Helen whispered to Yann, "What is he on about? Who are all these people?"

"All these people are Ossian, and Lee is flattering him. Let the faery use his fancy words. It is about all he can do."

Then a tall man, fair-haired and full of smiles, stood up. "I am Ossian. I forget my deeds, but those who arrive remind me of them occasionally. I will hear your tale, then you may ask your favour."

So Lee and Yann between them, with their light and deep voices, told of the tragedy of the child James stolen away, the worried mother, the lonely sister. They told of the wicked ways of the Faery Queen, and the quests and courage of the child fiddler that she wanted. Helen realized they meant her and hid, red-cheeked, behind Sapphire for a minute.

Then Yann, as tall as Ossian, with his hair like copper in the sunlight, asked the favour. "To free the stolen child tomorrow night, we need to provide the Faery Queen with music. We know of no better music than yours, and we know of no one else who could play for her, then get away unharmed afterwards. You have done it before, we ask that you do it one more time, to free the child she has, and to protect the child she wants."

Ossian laughed. "It sounds like good sport. But there will be a price to pay.

"We lack variety here, just as we lack bad weather. We never see rain and we rarely see new challenges either.

"I will come to your revels with my old harp and young fingers tomorrow. But only if you beat me and my companions in a few small contests first."

He considered the men lounging on the ground at his feet, then grinned at the group of children in front of him.

"I will put forward Tir nan Og's greatest hound and fastest runner. You must match them, to bring down a deer and bring the deer back. The runner who brings the deer back first wins.

"I will put forward Tir nan Og's greatest warrior and one of you must beat him in a duel.

"Finally, I myself will challenge you to a riddling contest.

"If you win all three contests, and brighten this long day for us, I will be your bard tomorrow night."

Helen and her friends formed a smaller version of the Fianna's circle.

"At least these aren't quests set by someone trying to trick us, these are honest competitions," urged Helen.

Lavender objected, "These men have hunted and fought their whole lives. How can we beat them?"

"I have hunted all my life," said Sylvie.

"I have trained to fight duels since I could hold a sword," said Lee.

Helen nodded. "What about the riddling?"

"You solved riddles for us last year," said Yann. "You can do it again."

So Helen turned to Ossian. "We accept your challenges."

Ossian smiled, his golden moustache waggling. "Let's go to the top of the hill and find the deer that graze on the moor. Then your hunter and your runner can compete against mine."

Helen asked as they climbed, "Sylvie can hunt a deer, but she can't carry one. Who will run the race?"

Yann laughed. "I will! Nothing on two legs can beat me."

They reached a grassy ridge overlooking a heathery moor, which was many times wider than the island they had flown over just minutes ago. On the moor, to their left, they saw the rusty red dots of a herd of deer.

Ossian said, "My hunter is the greatest hound that ever was. Here girl. Bran!"

Over the ridge bounded a massive deerhound: long-legged, long-bodied, snake-skulled. Built for running and leaping, chasing and killing.

"Who is your hunter?" asked Ossian.

"I am," said Sylvie. She flickered into a wolf more elegantly than Helen had ever seen. No half-beast girl in fur. Just a flurry of grey, then the wolf stood in front of them.

The dog Bran and the wolf Sylvie stared at each other.

Bran was taller in the shoulders, but skinnier, with a slight hunch to her lithe spine. Her sandy hair was wiry and coarse. Sylvie had a heavier jaw, bigger brighter eyes and her silver fur was longer and softer. They moved a step closer to each other. Sylvie's fur bristled. Bran's hackles rose. Ossian put his hand on Bran's back. Helen stood close to Sylvie.

"Now my runner," he said. "Caoilte, the fastest of the fleet Fianna, who can run from the north to the south to the east to the west so fast you are still speaking the words that sent him when he returns."

A tall man, skinny and pale, stepped out of the gathering of the Fianna, unpinned his cloak and gave it to the man on his left, then took a spear from the man on his right.

He flexed his long wiry legs. "Who will race me?"

"I will," said Yann.

Caoilte looked Yann up and down, examining his horse legs as if he was thinking of buying him. "I've never met a horse, not even a talking one, I couldn't beat."

Yann smiled confidently. "Then even on this land of forgetting, you can welcome a new experience!"

Ossian said, "The competitors have weighed each other's worth. Now let's see the quarry."

He pointed to the herd on the moor below. "This is a race not a fight, so I don't want you pursuing the same quarry. I don't want your teeth bared at each other.

"Bran and Caoilte, bring me the deer with the reddest hide.

"Wolf girl and horse boy, bring me the palest deer.

"The winner is the one who drops their quarry at my feet first.

"Go!"

He lifted his hand and slipped the hound at his side.

Helen expected to see Bran race off, Sylvie at her shoulder, in a desperate sprint downhill. But both hunting dogs, the wild and the tame, crouched low, bellies almost touching the earth, and slid downhill towards the herd in almost invisible forward movements. The runners didn't move at all.

Of course. Helen realized there was no point in either Bran or Sylvie getting to the grazing ground first if they'd already scared the deer away.

This might be the slowest race ever. Helen sat down to watch.

Chapter 17

As Bran and Sylvie raced slowly towards the herd, Caoilte and Yann stared at each other. Arms folded, legs relaxed. Neither in a hurry to begin the race.

Helen frowned. Was no one taking this seriously?

Lee smiled. "It's a stand off. Neither will admit they need to be near the kill to get back first; it would be a sign of weakness to leave first."

Helen shook her head, wondering if she'd ever understand boys.

She looked downhill. The wolf and the hound had disappeared from view.

Lavender whispered, "They're moving round to the left, so they can come at the deer downwind."

Helen looked to her left and saw two wriggles in the heather halfway down the hill.

The deer were still grazing happily.

Helen had a sudden desire to yell, or wave her arms, or throw a shoe at the herd, to warn them of the approaching danger. She clenched her fists in her pockets.

Yann and Caoilte broke off their staring match to glance down the hill. They nodded to each other. A friendly agreement. They both started walking very slowly.

Suddenly the world exploded into speed.

One of the deer lifted its head, sniffing the air … then it bolted.

The rest of the herd moved as one, sprinting across the moor.

The heather broke open at the foot of the ridge and two shapes shot out. Silver and gold, racing towards the deer.

The man and the centaur ran too.

But Helen didn't watch Yann and Caoilte. She watched the hound and the wolf. Normally, Helen supposed, they would go for the stragglers at the back of the herd, but on this hunt, they'd been given more difficult quarry.

They raced past a limping hind, who almost fell over her hooves in surprise at still being alive after being overtaken by a deerhound and a wolf. They followed the main body of the herd, the healthy fast animals.

They weren't running side by side any more. Bran was chasing a young stag, with small antlers and a rich red hide, along the foot of the ridge. Sylvie was pursuing a pale slim hind, who was leaping over heather and tiny burns, heading further into the moor.

Then the stag swerved and doubled back towards the grazing ground. Bran curved round to follow him.

Helen sighed. "Our hind is running further away, Bran's stag is coming back! Even if Sylvie brings the deer down, Yann will have much further to run than Caoilte."

Lavender groaned beside her. "Worse than that. She's chasing a white hind. A very lucky animal. It will not bring luck to our quest to kill a white hind."

Helen glanced at Ossian. Was he another tricky one? Had he set them up to fail too?

He was watching the hunt, whispering encouragement to Bran from under his long silky moustache.

Helen looked back down. Both deer were tiring, cut off from the protection of their herd. The wolf and the hound seemed to have endless energy in their long springy legs.

Helen felt a shudder of guilt. Sylvie and Bran were hunting live animals, terrifying them, chasing them to their death, as a sport, to decide if Ossian would play to protect her. These deer were being sacrificed for her and James.

She couldn't let that happen.

She shifted in the heather, starting to get up. Lee put his hand on her knee. "They are predators, Helen. This is what they do. They hunt. Sylvie hunts to eat. She hunted yesterday. She will hunt tomorrow. She's not doing this for you, she's doing this because she is a wolf. You don't need to feel guilty."

Helen nodded reluctantly. She knew Sylvie didn't buy her meals in the supermarket, those fangs weren't just for frightening people, but it was still hard to watch her hunt.

Sylvie wasn't behind the pale deer now. She was running beside her.

Bran had reached the hindquarters of the stag.

Sylvie came alongside the hind's head and leapt for her neck. The weight and speed of the wolf knocked the deer to the ground.

An instant later, Bran brought the stag down, her teeth gripping his throat. Caoilte caught up with them and stabbed his spear down.

Helen closed her eyes. Then opened them again. Where was Yann?

He was already with Sylvie. Pulling the hind onto his shoulders and galloping towards the ridge.

Caoilte dropped his spear and hauled the stag onto his bony shoulders.

Helen said anxiously, "Yann has a longer distance to run!"

Lavender pointed out, "Their runner has a heavier burden."

Lee added, "And Yann has more legs."

The race between Yann and Caoilte had been preceded by stares and begun with a nod, but now it was run in earnest.

Helen had never seen Yann gallop at such speed. Nor had she ever seen a man run so fast. But on the flat Yann was faster. They could hear the boom of his hooves on the earth, while Caoilte ran silently on his hard bare feet.

They reached the base of the ridge at the same time, but Caoilte was directly beneath Ossian. Yann was out to his right, with further to go uphill. He had won the sprint; could he win the climb?

Caoilte ran straight up the ridge, the stag bouncing on his shoulders, deer blood running down his chest. Yann, whose horse legs were not designed for scrambling, was struggling across the slope lower down, his hooves scraping and his breath heaving.

The big men of the Fianna laughed, taunting their companion. "He's catching up, Caoilte. Can't you smell his horse sweat? Don't you remember how to win? Perhaps you should have hunted a hare not a deer, it would be lighter." Only Ossian, standing apart like a judge, wasn't yelling.

Lee called out, "Yann! You have the power of a stallion and the pride of a warrior. You have won the race of the flat as a horse, now win the race of the hill as a man!"

Lavender joined in, though Yann couldn't hear her over the noise of his hooves and breath. "You're the fastest fabled beast on any island!"

Sapphire sent up a beacon of sparks for him to run towards.

Helen shouted, "You will be our first victory, Yann, on our first successful quest!"

The Fianna laughed louder. "The boy has horseflies as fans, Caoilte! Can you hear them buzzing? Come up here and silence them."

But it was too late for Caoilte. While everyone searched for the right words to goad or encourage their runner, Yann found more breath, more power, more speed. He leapt the last few rocks and shot past the groaning Caoilte. He dropped his burden, a pale crumpled heap, at the feet of Ossian.

Yann tottered three more steps, then leant against Sapphire's wide strong side, so he didn't fall to the ground.

Helen ran to him. "Thank you so much."

Then she ran to the deer.

Ossian now had two deer at his feet. Caoilte, who was making a show of staying on his feet without support, had just dropped a bloody heap of red hide and antlers beside the splayed legs and white hide of Sylvie's prey.

But when Helen looked at the hind, she couldn't see any blood. She bent down. The white hind was still breathing. Helen stroked her soft muzzle and the huge long-lashed eyes opened, just as Sylvie and Bran slunk over the edge of the ridge.

Sylvie slid over to Yann and smudged weakly back into a girl.

The white hind sprang to her feet.

Helen stroked the deer's muzzle again. She felt the deer's warm breath on her hand.

The hind trotted down the hill.

Ossian laughed. "The luckiest animal on Tir nan Og has blessed you, child. I wonder if your luck will hold with the next contest."

Helen turned to Sylvie. "Did you know you hadn't killed her? Did you plan to let her live?"

Sylvie coughed. "I listen to bargains much better than you, human child. I was challenged to bring her down, not to kill her. I wasn't going to kill a white hind; it would have been a very inauspicious start to this quest. So I just knocked her down. But she led me a good hunt first."

Helen laughed in relief. "Poor thing. She didn't know you weren't planning to rip her throat out. Yann would have had a shorter distance to race if you'd told her your plans. She wouldn't have run so far, so fast, if she hadn't been in fear of her life."

"That would have been cheating. Anyway, only a

foolish deer would trust the word of a wolf." Sylvie grinned, showing her sharp white teeth.

Ossian nodded seriously. "First round to the challengers from the sky. Now, let's go down to the flat grass and see how you fare with weapons. Who is your swordsman?"

"I am," said Lee, flipping back his cloak, a brighter, more confident scarlet than any red the Fianna wore.

"You must face Cuchullin, the champion of all Celtic warriors. Are you ready to do that for your fiddler and your small boy?"

Lee laid his hand on his hilt. "I am always ready."

They followed the Fianna down the hill. Only Helen glanced back at the red stag lying on the ridge.

Yann finally found enough breath to speak. He put his hand on Lee's shoulder. "Lil …" he shook his head. "Lee. Thank you for your words of encouragement."

Lee shrugged gently, allowing the centaur's hand to stay on his shoulder. "You ran brilliantly. You just needed a warm welcome, not the thorns the Fianna were throwing under Caoilte's feet."

Yann tightened his grip on the faery's shoulder. "Now I want to give you words of warning. All I did was run a race, Lee. There was no danger to me, nor Sylvie. Just a hard race.

"But you face a fight. A fight against the legendary warrior those mountains we flew past were named after. The legendary warrior so fierce in battle they run three baths of ice-cold water to cool him when his enemies are dead. When he jumps into the first bath it steams away to nothing, the second bubbles and boils, the third simmers, because his battle rage burns so hot.

"You take too much of a risk facing Cuchullin. You could be injured, you could be killed. There must be another sport we can play to persuade Ossian to help Helen."

"You just won a race against the fastest man in myth! But you think I should back away from my challenge?"

"I think you're young and untried. Cuchullin is a champion."

"So am I," Lee grinned. "I am my King's champion."

"You have a title, but what does it mean? It means your King asked you to spy for him, to intrigue against his wife, to help a human child. Champion is a title to give you confidence. It doesn't make you a warrior. It shouldn't get you killed."

"It's not an honorary title. It's not a bauble given to friends or loyal servants. You have to earn the title of champion."

"How?" asked Helen, walking fast to keep up. "How do you earn it?"

"You have to kill the previous champion," Lee said harshly.

He strode down the hill. Helen's step faltered. She let him get ahead.

The Fianna led them back to the river, to a circle of grass, not green and lush like the rest of the riverbank, but trampled flat.

Lee took off his hat, his cloak and his waistcoat, and laid them carefully on a clean rock at the edge of the circle. Soon the faery was wearing only his breeches, his shirt, his boots and the belt holding his scabbard.

Ossian summoned the island's champion. "Cuchullin! I have a duel for you to fight."

Helen saw a figure walk towards them from a grove of rowan trees. Tall. Broad. And terrifying.

He looked permanently angry. His face scowled. His bristly red hair stood on end. One of his eyes bulged huge and red-rimmed, the other was half-closed in a painful squint. His lips were drawn back, showing his crooked yellow teeth.

"My lord, who do you want me to kill?"

Ossian pointed at Lee.

Chapter 18

"I want you to kill this one," Ossian said smoothly to Cuchullin. "The faery. Kill him or disarm him, disable him or ground him, my champion, or else I must work again. We of the ever young do not work, do we?"

"Except me," muttered Cuchullin. "I work every time I lift the sword for you."

Ossian smiled. "But you love it. So do it for me one more time."

Cuchullin pulled his shield off his back, dragged the pin from the neck of his cloak and threw the cloak on the ground. He marched grumpily towards Lee, who was standing in the centre of the trampled grass, his shoulders relaxed inside his perfectly white, uncreased shirt.

Cuchullin stopped suddenly and looked in disbelief

at his opponent. "You want me to fight this child? This pup? This flea on the neck of the runt of the litter?"

Ossian laughed. "He wants to fight you."

"He doesn't even have a shield. I can't fight a child without a shield."

"I don't need a shield," said Lee calmly. "My sword is my defence."

"You will wear a shield on one arm and hold a sword with the other," insisted Cuchullin. "It's the way a man fights. I will teach you that, before I teach you how to fight, then teach you how to lose."

Lee smiled politely. "I have no shield with me."

"I will lend you one."

The Fianna's circle broke into a flurry of activity, with shields tossed around and weighed and compared. A round wooden shield, covered in leather and with a bronze boss in the centre, was thrown at Lee's feet.

Lee picked it up, slid the leather handles at the back over his left arm and said, "I have been ready all this time. Are you ready yet?"

Cuchullin nodded as he walked towards Lee.

Lee's shield was large enough to cover him from the top of his thighs to his throat. Cuchullin's oval shield was even longer. Helen hoped that meant it would be heavier.

Cuchullin was taller and wider than Lee. His arms bulged with muscles, where Lee's were slim and smooth. Cuchullin's sword was longer and broader, though Lee's sword shone brighter.

Helen had seen the faery polish and sharpen that blade. The gleam on his weapon wasn't glamour or enchantment. It was love and care and pride.

Helen hoped his pride wasn't misplaced. Lee was about to risk his life to save her and James from the Faery Queen. Could she let him do that? But before she'd reached the end of the thought, the fight had started.

Helen thought duels began with insults, circling, flourishes of the blade, but there were no preliminaries. As Cuchullin reached the centre of the circle, he raised his sword and slashed across Lee's throat, in a blow that would have sliced the faery's head off if he hadn't spun away.

Lee slashed back, over the rim of his borrowed shield. Cuchullin, instead of dodging the blow, moved into it, took the force of it on his own shield and crashed into Lee, using his weight and height and longer shield to force Lee backwards and downwards.

But Lee was no longer there. Shorter and faster, he had twisted away again.

Helen thought they were fighting more with their shields than their swords. Battering the metal centres together. Slicing the sharp edges at each other's faces and knees. Driving them hard with their shoulders into each other's bodies.

Then they realized that the shields would not break, though the leather covering was ripped, and that their weight would not wear down their opponent. So the shields became, not weapons, but instruments of deceit.

By hiding their sword hands behind the shields, both Lee and Cuchullin could hide the direction of the sword's next attack behind a counter motion of the shield.

Lee stabbed his blade over the top rim and Cuchullin

fell to his knees to avoid the point arcing towards his face.

Cuchullin, quickly back on his feet, brought the edge of his blade out from under his shield and slashed at Lee's legs. The red leather of the faery's right boot flapped open as the blade slid along it.

"Below the belt!" muttered Helen. "Aren't there any rules?"

"Yes," said Yann. "Don't die first."

They spoke quietly. Everyone else was silent, listening to the sounds of the fight. The thump of feet on the ground. The thud of shields meeting edge to edge, boss to boss. The whistle as blades moved fast through the air. The crash and the echoes of the crash as blades smashed together.

She watched Lee's sword snake out from the edge of the shield and attack Cuchullin again.

"What's he fighting with?" she whispered.

"Every skill he has," Yann whispered back.

"No, I meant the sword. You know he can't touch iron. So what's his sword made of?"

"Bronze. The faeries use bronze swords, spearheads and knives."

"Bronze?" repeated Helen. "Like the bronze age? Like axes in museums? Lee is fighting with a prehistoric weapon?"

She watched his slim figure twist out of the way of a slashing drive. Lee's sword was as sharp and lethal-looking as Cuchullin's weapon.

Yann grinned. "Some of your people's greatest warriors fought with bronze. Achilles and Hector fought by the walls of Troy with bronze blades."

Helen watched as the two blades met with a clatter above the fighters' heads. Was Lee's sword more coppery red than the silver steel of Cuchullin's sword? Or was that just the sun reflecting on it?

Sylvie laughed grimly. "If Lee can drive his blade into that man, it will kill him just as dead as iron or steel."

But as the duel continued, it didn't look like Lee was going to have the chance, or the strength, to prove the value of his blade.

Lee had been faster to start with, but he was tiring now. His face was grey, his breath audible even over the grunts of the angry swordsman.

And Lee wasn't bringing his sword out from the safety of the shield any more. He wasn't even using the shield as a weapon, just as a hiding place. He was sheltering under it, while the blade of Cuchullin crashed down and down and down like a joiner hammering nails into wood.

Helen said, "He's going to be killed. We must stop this. It isn't worth his life, to save mine."

"Don't humiliate him by interfering," Yann ordered. "It was his choice to fight. You have to respect that."

"No," interrupted Lavender from Helen's shoulder. "It wasn't all his choice. It wasn't his choice to fight with that shield. Take this bandage off, I need to get closer."

Helen quickly unwound the narrow bandage. Lavender extended her wings to fly up and over the duel, listing to the left as she struggled to use her painful wing, but staying so high that neither fighter saw her.

Then she fluttered back, falling into Helen's cupped hands. "I knew something wasn't right. It's the shield. Look next time Lee turns. Where the leather is torn at the edge. What do you see?"

Lee swivelled right round and Helen stared hard. Where the brown hide was ripped, she could see nails holding the wooden boards together. They weren't the brassy bronze of the boss, but a darker metal.

Lavender worked it out first and yelled at the top of her tiny voice. "Iron! Lee! The shield has iron on it!"

Lee was breathing loudly, and the crash of the sword on the shield was like a marching drum, and Cuchullin was muttering angrily under his breath. Lavender's voice was as small as her body and Lee didn't hear her warning.

So Helen opened her mouth to yell.

But Yann rose onto his hind legs, using his stallion's lungs and his storyteller's voice to scream, "Lee! Drop the shield! Now!"

Lee heard a voice he trusted and obeyed instantly. He didn't look round at the centaur, he didn't glance at the shield. He just flung the shield away, spinning it along the ground to Sapphire's feet.

Suddenly without protection, he had to somersault out of the way of the next sword slash and leap to his feet, struggling to catch his breath.

Then he stood up straight, his sword steady in his pale hand.

Cuchullin laughed. "Was the shield weighing you down, faery? Then let's both fight light and fast." He threw his shield away too, crashing it into the smaller one at the dragon's feet. She put her claws on the edge of the oval shield, as if she was about to tiddlywink the round one into the river beside her.

The fight began again. It sounded different now. Lee's breathing was lighter, less laboured. Their feet moved faster. There was no deep drumbeat of shield music. Just the light sharp notes of blade against blade, iron against bronze.

Now they fought in sudden bursts. Without shields, they couldn't stay so close. Instead they rushed forward to attack and jumped back to defend.

Lee would run forward and attack Cuchullin, who would parry and knock him back. Then they would circle each other, watching their opponents' eyes and blades, until one or other would leap to the attack again.

They were using more of the ground, fighting beside the campfire and the riverbank, as well as in the centre of the circle.

Lee had his colour back, and most of his speed. But he wasn't grinning, unlike Cuchullin, whose grunts and growls weren't so angry now. "Even without the iron sickness, you are no match for me, faery boy."

Lee didn't answer, he just attacked again, driving at Cuchullin's chest. His sword was knocked sideways, his guard down for a moment, and Cuchullin pointed his sword at Lee's throat.

Lee brought his own sword back and parried the menacing point, but Cuchullin circled it round and pointed at Lee's throat again.

The faery stepped back as the man moved towards him along the bank of the river, forcing the point ever forward. Lee pushed it away again, but not far and not for long, and the point got nearer and nearer to his throat.

Then Lee brought his sword up and round and down, hard and fast, and drove the threatening sword all the way to the ground. But the clang of the two blades meeting sounded flat and wrong. Helen saw the coppery blade of Lee's sword shiver. He used his left hand to grab and support his right wrist, shaken and shocked by the impact.

Lee backed off and looked along the length of his sword. He frowned.

He backed off further, rubbing his aching wrist.

Helen tried to run forward, to protect Lee. Yann blocked her way with a heavy hoof. "Don't. You can't help him now."

Lee backed away a few more steps. Trailing the tip of his damaged sword.

Falling backwards, struggling to stay on his feet. The flap of his cut boot dragging on the ground, the tip of his sword getting dusty in the earth.

His face pale, his steps slow, Lee kept backing away.

Chapter 19

Cuchullin screamed his triumph. "See the true value of iron! Steel against bronze will always win!"

He laughed, as Lee backed further away.

Then he raised his sword and aimed it at Lee's throat one last time.

"Are you going to run, boy?"

"Yes," said Lee quietly.

Yann groaned in disappointment.

And Lee ran.

He ran towards the tall red-headed warrior.

He lifted his sword delicately and sprinted straight at the steady blade of Cuchullin.

But at the last moment, when Cuchullin's blade and arm were fixed immovably at the point Lee was running towards, Lee swerved and leapt into the air, raising his sword, crashing the broad hilt into Cuchullin's face, jabbing his twisting elbow into Cuchullin's throat. Then he flung himself aside as the grey blade slashed up and the man fell backwards into the river.

Water spouted into the air like steam from a kettle. Water whirled white round Cuchullin like boiling bubbles in a pan.

When the water settled, Lee was standing in the river, the tip of his sword on the belly of his enemy, his left hand resting on the pommel, ready to drive the sword down.

"No!" yelled Helen, running towards them. "Stop!"

Ossian stood on the bank. "Well fought. Well won."

Lee nodded and lifted the sword high into the air.

Yann reached down from the bank and pulled Lee out of the water. Then Lee leant down and offered his hand to Cuchullin, who accepted it and scrambled out of the river. A friend threw him his cloak and he hid his bright red face and wet red hair in it as he dried himself.

"Lee!" cried Helen. "Why didn't you refuse the shield? You must have known it had iron in it. Iron always makes you feel sick. Why did you take it?"

"I didn't know it was iron." Lee leant down, trying to put his boot back together. "I did feel really sick and sweaty when I took the shield, but I thought it was because he was walking towards me. I thought it was because I was scared."

Yann slapped his back. "You didn't look scared, my friend. You looked like a King's champion … and you fought like one too."

The two of them grinned at each other. Helen shook her head.

They all walked back to the Fianna's fire, Sapphire putting every one of her clawed feet carefully on the round shield which had nearly killed Lee, leaving it crushed to splinters behind her.

"Not again!" said Lee, as the leather on his fancy red boot flapped loose. Suddenly he was walking beside Helen in a pair of squelching trainers and damp jeans with a rip in the left leg.

Sylvie gasped, Yann laughed, Lavender muttered disapprovingly, "That won't go with the waistcoat and cloak," and Helen finally managed to smile.

The men of the Fianna made space for the centaur, the wolf, the faery and the fiddler to sit round the fire. There wasn't quite enough room for the dragon, who lay in a curve behind her friends, picking bits of shield out from between her toes.

Ossian spoke sternly to the damp Cuchullin. "Giving a faery a shield to protect him, with iron studs to undermine him. Was that honourable?"

Cuchullin looked sourly at Ossian. "I took my cue from you, my lord, setting the wolf to hunt the white hind. Was that sportsman-like?"

"All they stood to lose from my trick was a hunt. The boy was losing his life with your shield over his heart." Ossian shook his head. "But he won, so that is the second task to the young challengers.

"Now, who will answer my three riddles?"

Helen said, "We'll answer them together."

"No. Your boy fought alone. Your wolf hunted, and your horse raced, alone. Your bard will answer alone."

Helen took a deep breath. "Alright. I will answer."

Ossian smiled. "You must reply to my riddles not just

with truth, because the bare truth is too harsh, you must reply also with beauty. That's the way to turn a riddle into a poem."

Helen sighed. She didn't tell stories with exciting words like Yann and Sylvie, or declaim in fancy words like Lee, or cast spells with clever words like Lavender, or stop quarrels with wise words like Sapphire. Perhaps she shouldn't have volunteered for this.

Ossian stared at Helen through smoke rising into the blue sky, and asked his first riddle.

"What is more precious than yellow gold and worth more than white diamonds?"

Helen sighed. Would an answer about bank accounts and oil pipelines work here on Tir nan Og? She doubted it. She must give an answer that would be understandable in the Fianna's world.

She looked around, hoping for inspiration.

All her friends were staring at her. Lavender was sitting on Sylvie's head, tiny hands clamped over her mouth, afraid to come closer in case she was accused of cheating. Helen turned to her left, and saw Lee look quickly behind her.

She glanced back. Sapphire was using a claw to ping an old necklace Helen had given her against the shiny scales of her left leg. The necklace was a bit tatty now, but Sapphire still wore it as a sign of their friendship.

Helen grinned, then turned back. But the right answer wasn't enough. She needed beauty as well as truth.

"More precious than gold and diamonds..." What was the exact question? She mouthed it to herself, then she thought how Yann would answer it when he was being pompous.

"More precious than yellow gold and worth more than white diamonds, are the friends you can trust with your treasure."

Ossian laughed. "Nicely put, for one surrounded by helpful friends!

"My second riddle. What drink is hot and sweet and salty, all at once?"

Helen made a face, remembering the time she had tipped a sachet of salt into her hot chocolate in a café. That probably wasn't the answer Ossian was looking for.

She glanced at the group around her again. Yann, Lee and Lavender were staring at Sylvie, who was licking her lips. Helen frowned. Sylvie bared her teeth and swallowed.

Helen raised her eyebrows and thought hard. Then she spoke, "Hot and sweet and salt, all at once, is the blood from fresh caught prey."

Sylvie laughed and hugged Helen. "You do understand!"

Ossian said pointedly, "This third riddle is for you alone.

"What is the most beautiful music?"

Helen didn't even look round; she knew the truth of this riddle herself. But how could she answer it for Ossian's ears? It needed a longer answer than the ones she had managed up until now.

She remembered how Lee had spoken to Ossian when they first arrived, how his list of titles and names had sounded like a poem or song. That list might give her a structure, but what words should she use?

She had spent so much time with her fabled friends, listening to their flowing, flowery, formal language. Could she copy it convincingly?

Then she realized it would be like playing a tune in the style of a musician she admired. She closed her eyes for a moment, remembering the rhythm of Lee's speech and the melody of Yann's words.

She started to speak in a voice so soft it was almost a whisper:

"The most beautiful music is:

"For a mother the laugh of a baby in her arms,

"For a warrior the whine of a blade in the air,

"For a sailor the wind whistling through the ropes,

"For a hunter the baying of hounds on the hill,

"For a miser the clink of coins in a bag,

"For a host the belches of his well-fed guests,

"And for a bard, the moment of silence before the applause, the cheers and the encores."

After a moment of silence, Ossian spoke. "Beauty, truth and a riddle of your own. What is an encore?"

"An encore," Helen answered carefully, "is when the audience love your music so much they ask you to play again. Just like we're asking the greatest bard ever to play just one more time."

She stopped. She had said enough.

Ossian frowned, then laughed. "Neatly done. You win the contest and offer me a gracious way to pay the forfeit.

"Where and when do you wish me to play to save your young boy, what was his name again? And what do you wish me to bring?"

Helen could hardly answer, she was shivering with

relief. Their quest had been successful. They had found their bard.

Helen said, "Please come to the green hill in the west of Dorry Shee an hour before midnight tomorrow night. Bring your harp and your heroism, to save James and escape yourself. And bring some good dancing tunes too!"

Suddenly they were going home.

Ossian said goodbye to them all, hugging Yann and Lee, slapping Sapphire on her rump, and clasping wrists in a handshake with Sylvie. He just smiled at Lavender, who was too small for a hearty Fianna farewell.

He looked at Helen. "Thank you for good sport and for the chance to see midsummer's night one more time. I give you my word that I will be there."

Helen saw Sylvie kneel down beside Bran, so her eyes were on a level with the hound. Did they nod at each other?

Then the men of the Fianna gave them all boosts onto the dragon's back, and Sapphire was airborne again.

She flew straight upwards into a cloud that cast no shadow on Tir nan Og, then turned east. Once they were out of the greyness of the cloud, all they could see was the dark sea below and the faint bruised stripes of an old sunset behind.

Once they reached the mainland, Sapphire flew south-east until they arrived at Dorry Shee, where Lee and Yann had a competition to see who could chuck sandwiches most accurately into a root cave from the back of a dragon. Then they were near their own clearing, falling off the dragon's back in a happy tangle of legs and wings and hooves.

Helen yelled, "We did it! Our own quest! And we did it!

"You were all wonderful. Racing, hunting, fighting and giving me answers. We did it together."

She hugged them all.

"Now we have our bard, and Ossian will be more than a match for the Queen tomorrow!"

She sat down, waiting for her heartbeat to slow. Yann and Lee were comparing scratches and scrapes from their race and fight. Helen didn't bother with the first aid kit; they seemed more proud of their injuries than bothered by them.

Lavender was adjusting the necklace on Sapphire's leg. But Sylvie stood quietly on the edge of the group, her head down, her shoulders hunched. Helen went over to her.

"You were wonderful. You brought a deer down, then didn't even taste her hot sweet salty blood, just to preserve our luck. That was amazing. Thank you, Sylvie."

Sylvie looked at Helen, her face pale and pointed. "Now what, human child?"

"Now, we get James back. And the Faery Queen won't get her real live music forever, because no one can hold onto Ossian."

"She will still have her party," growled Sylvie. "With the greatest bard ever, she will have the greatest party ever, so the faeries who come will never leave … and we will have lost our forest. *And I have helped you do it!*"

She almost howled in frustration and misery.

Helen shook her head. "The party hasn't been a success yet. They haven't settled in your forest yet.

"I promise, once we have the boy safe, we will help you protect your land against the faeries. I know we failed in one quest, but it was set up by the Queen. Our own quest was a complete success. If we set ourselves the task of driving your enemies away, I'm sure we can do it.

"We free James, then it's open season on faery parties."

"Do you have a plan, human child?"

"Not yet."

"When will you have a plan?"

"Em ... soon? Tomorrow?"

Sylvie shook her head. "You will never have a plan. You're just making this up as you go along. That's why it was so easy for the Queen to give you a quest which you flung yourself into and failed. That's why you needed every single one of us to win you your bard. You're making it up as you go along."

Helen stayed silent. Sylvie was probably right.

"Any success you have is entirely accidental." The wolf-girl spoke sharply. "But tomorrow, your success could be my failure. I will not go back to my pack a failure. So if you don't have a plan to save my forest, as well as your boy, by the time your bard arrives tomorrow night, then my brothers and I will stop the party by preventing your musician playing. With our teeth and claws if we have to."

Helen looked round. No one was laughing and joking now.

They were all questing for different prizes. And they hadn't beaten the Faery Queen yet.

Chapter 20

Helen sat down, her legs suddenly weak with exhaustion.

Lavender fluttered over to comfort her, crash-landing into her forehead. The fairy's flying was still erratic. Helen stuck her hand out and caught the falling fairy.

Lavender rolled over on Helen's palm and said, "Don't worry. We all need a good night's sleep and a nice hot breakfast, then we'll think of something."

Yann said confidently. "We will meet before either Ossian or the summer school musicians arrive at the mound tomorrow, and come up with the plan Sylvie needs. Ossian might even help."

"We must stop the summer school coming to the forest at all," Sylvie snapped.

"No," insisted Helen. "Fay Greenhill must be communicating with the Faery Queen somehow. So we need to act like I'm sacrificing the school for James, which is what she's expecting me to do, or else she'll come up with other tricks."

"But we *do* have to stop the summer school going into the mound. How can we do that?" asked Lavender.

"My brothers would be happy to pin them down." Sylvie ran her tongue over her sharp front teeth.

Helen said, "No! We don't want them going home with tales of wolves in Dorry Shee, bringing hunters and film crews back with them.

"We need to get Ossian inside first, then James out, then I can tell the summer school folk that the concert has been cancelled, or moved, or postponed."

They refined the plan a little, with Yann volunteering to ride back to the cottage with the boy once he was freed, and Lee, Sylvie and Sapphire arguing about the best vantage point for keeping an eye both on the minibus's parking space at the forest edge and the green mound within the trees.

Helen drifted into a doze as she waited for her friends to decide where and when to meet. Yann woke her with a nudge. "I'll take you home."

She clambered onto his back, yawning, and he broke into a trot. Helen looked up. Through ragged clouds, she saw the bear and eagle stars watching them. "Slow down, the Wild Hunt might be out tonight."

So the centaur walked her home, not much faster than she could have walked herself.

Helen looked behind occasionally. She didn't see any red-eared dogs or any wolves. But her neck was prickling and she wondered if Sylvie's brothers were watching her, waiting for her to fail again.

When they got back to the lodge, Helen jumped down. "Thanks for the company, Yann. See you tomorrow."

Yann's face was bright in the light from the buildings. He took a step backwards, but didn't leave. He cleared his throat. "Don't bring your fiddle."

"Pardon?"

"When you come tomorrow, don't bring your fiddle."

"Why not?"

"Because if you don't have it, you can't play for them."

"I'm not going to play for them. Ossian is. Anyway, all the summer school students will have their instruments, so it'll look really strange if I leave mine at home. I have to take it."

"Helen. Promise me you won't bring it."

"You're hoping that if I don't have my fiddle, when Ossian has his harp, and the students have their pipes, flutes, fiddles and drums, then I'll be the only human there safe from the Faery Queen. That even if I'm tempted, I won't be able to play for her."

"Yes."

"I can't do that. That would be … unfair. Cheating."

"It would be sensible. Please leave your fiddle at home."

Helen smiled wearily at him, shook her head, then trudged towards the lodge. The cottage was dark. So was the Professor's bedroom window. The four wings were still brightly lit, and she heard competing threads of melody, as nervous students over-rehearsed.

Helen went straight to bed. She had neither the energy nor the desire to rehearse.

Next morning, Helen joined the rest of the Murray Wing students for breakfast. It was her turn to make toast again, according to Zoe, which Juliet thought was unfair, as no one had made breakfast for Helen yet. Helen just shrugged. She wasn't going to bother making sandwiches today. James would either be free tonight or with the faeries forever, so she might as well use her bread-spreading skills for breakfast rather than picnics.

She barely spoke to anyone. She was thinking too hard, patching together everything she knew about faeries' weaknesses.

Could Ossian smuggle iron into the green hill? No, he would need to be inside before the boy got out and if the faeries sensed the iron too early, they would refuse to let the boy go.

Could he smuggle something else in? What? Helen had a sudden vision of itching powder and plastic spiders at an elegant faery party. She shook her head.

She wasn't even sure if Ossian would help them drive the faeries away. The bargain had only been for music. But could they do it on their own, without a hero? The Queen had run circles round them so far. Except last night. They had managed fine on their own last night. She grinned.

"What are you so pleased about?" Zoe snapped.

Helen glanced up. Everyone was staring at her.

"I'm looking forward to learning from your masterly solo performance tonight, Zoe." Helen smiled, knowing Ossian would be the only one playing a solo tonight, then put four more slices in the toaster.

After breakfast, they had a final full rehearsal. The Professor made them run through the beginning a dozen times.

"It is very important that you make a good impression,"

she said anxiously. "This is a very discerning audience. They will only stay until the end if you make the opening bars the best you have ever played. So let's try that one more time."

They tried it six more times and it was perfect every time, but the Professor flounced off on her spiky orange heels, saying perhaps she should write a simpler introduction.

Dr Lermontov smiled as she left the barn. "She is always nervous before a performance. Don't worry, she won't change it now. You have played brilliantly, all of you. Now you need to rest your fingers and your minds, so why not make yourselves a picnic and enjoy this sunny day … but don't go into the forest. We don't want to lose any of you before tonight. Even your soft Scottish forests could be dangerous."

"What do you mean," said Helen indignantly, "even our soft Scottish forests?"

"In Russia, we hide all our scariest things in the forest: child-eating witches and child-freezing frost fathers, as well as wolves and bears. But even in your fragrant Scottish forest, you could fall and sprain a wrist, or get lost and wander in circles.

"So take your sandwiches, sit on the rocks or by the water, but don't go into the trees."

Helen left the barn, made yet another picnic, then went to the cottage. Emma was sitting quietly at the table, looking red-eyed and lonely. Mrs McGregor was sitting on the couch, beside James, who was lying silent, still and very pale, with his cold eyes finally closed.

"How is he?" asked Helen.

"He hasn't spoken or moved since last night. The

doctor visited this morning and says she can't find anything wrong with him, but if James doesn't wake up and talk to me today, I'm going to take him to the hospital in Inverness tomorrow. I know he's not right. I need to get him some help."

Helen put her hand on the little boy's head. The skin was cold and hard. She leant closer. Did he smell of sawdust?

Helen said reassuringly, "It's midsummer night. A magical night. I know he will wake up tonight. I'm sure of it."

Mrs McGregor smiled weakly. "I hope you're right."

Helen stood up. "I've made a picnic. Would Emma like to share it with me?"

Emma looked up. "Chocolate biscuits?"

"Of course."

So Helen and Emma sat a little way from the sad cottage, ate chocolate biscuits, a whole packet between them, and threw stones into a small burn running down to the loch.

There were groups of summer school students lounging about in the heather and on the rocky shore of the loch. The sun shone, butterflies and dragonflies fluttered just out of reach, and almost everyone except Emma was too hot and happy to do more than lie still, eat and drink, chat and dream.

Helen stood on a wall and looked round. She could count all the pipers, fiddlers and drummers. If it went well tonight, every single one of them would be safe from the Faery Queen for ever.

From the wall, she watched Emma splashing barefoot on the pebbles of the burn.

Then she looked towards the forest edge. Was anyone watching from there? Her friends? The wolf people? The faeries? She jumped off the wall and sat in its shade; not hiding, just keeping cool.

Emma ran up and put a wet hand on Helen's nose. "Catch me a sticky fish!"

"A what?"

"James catches me sticky fish!"

"A sticky fish? Do you mean sticklebacks?"

"Yes! He catches them for me. Will you catch me one?"

"Sorry, I don't have a net. But James will catch you another one soon."

"James is too sleepy."

"James will wake up soon and catch lots of sticky fish."

"Promise?"

"Yes. I promise. James will wake up tonight and play with you tomorrow."

Helen jumped back on the wall and waved at the forest. She didn't care who saw her. She would go back into the forest tonight and get James out. She had promised.

Chapter 21

No one had seen Professor Greenhill since the morning rehearsal, so when Dr Lermontov announced at teatime that they would be leaving at 11pm to drive to the concert venue, Helen took a risk and put up her hand.

"Professor Greenhill asked me to be her runner tonight, so she's picking me up and taking me to the venue earlier. I won't be in the minibus with you, but I'll meet you there. The Professor said to let you know, so you didn't worry."

"You won't be in the forest on your own, will you?" he asked.

"Oh? Is the venue in the forest?" Helen asked innocently.

He frowned. "You won't be in there on your own, will you, Helen Strange?"

She thought about the wolves who had been watching her all week. "No, I never seem to be on my own."

But it wasn't the Professor who came to get her at 10 o'clock. It was Sapphire.

Helen stood at the back of the lodge and saw a jagged shape land on the track ahead of her. She ran over and leapt onto the dragon.

For the first time all week, Helen wasn't taking the first aid kit with her to the forest. Instead she was wearing her fiddle on her back. As they flew low along the glen, she felt the hard case press on her spine.

She loved her fiddle. She hoped it would be her violin for the rest of her life. It had a gorgeous gleam, a great sound and she knew its every foible: the notes it played perfectly, the notes you had to nurse and nurture out of it, and where its wolf note was. It was the gateway to the greatest joy she knew: performing music.

Right now, however, her fiddle felt very heavy. So heavy she was surprised Sapphire could lift it off the ground. For a moment, Helen was so scared of the night's possibilities, she wanted to take the violin case off and drop it to the ground below. But she knew she couldn't.

She couldn't imagine a life without music. Wherever she had to play.

Anyway, her fiddle was no danger to her tonight. Who would want Helen Strang to play her fiddle, when Ossian of the Fianna was playing his harp?

Far to the west of their usual meeting place, Sapphire landed on a steep ridge, with trees down one slope, and bare ground down the other.

Her friends had chosen this point well. Looking down in the late evening light, Helen saw the end of the track leading along the forest edge. This was as far as the lodge's minibus would come in an hour's time. Behind them, over the ridge and through the trees, was the green mound.

She started to slide down Sapphire's scales. The dragon smelt spicy and gleamed beautifully, so Helen guessed Lavender had been nervous and had spent most of the day polishing her friend with scented oils. It made the dragon smooth and slippy, and Helen skidded down faster than she meant to.

Yann and Lee grabbed her arms to stop her flying down the ridge.

Yann spun her round and looked at her back. "No first aid kit? Just the fiddle?"

"There won't be any quests, fights, or injuries tonight. We won't need first aid."

"You won't need the fiddle either."

"I hope not." Helen swung the case off her back and laid it carefully on a tree stump.

Sylvie walked right up to her, and stood just a little too close. "What's your plan to drive the faeries from my forest?"

Helen looked up. "It's cloudy tonight, which is good, because we won't have to worry about the Wild Hunt, but there's bound to be another cloudless night soon. So when the starry hunters are hungry, if the Queen's still here, she'll hunt again.

"And we'll be ready. We'll lay a trail of aniseed, like drag hunters use instead of real foxes, and lure the hounds of the Wild Hunt to circle round and come up behind the faery hunters. So the Wild Hunt will chase itself out of the forest…"

Lee laughed. "That's very neat! I must make sure none of my friends hunt that night, because that will take a few of your lifetimes to sort out!"

Sylvie growled. "I don't know. Will the hounds follow aniseed?"

Helen shrugged. "Most hunting dogs do, but the most important thing is they chase running prey, so we must stay still and let the faeries do the running. You must say the same to your pack.

"So, Sylvie. Do you like my plan? Will you help us tonight?"

Sylvie grunted. "It's just as ridiculous and unworkable as everything else you've done this week, so I suppose it's just as likely to turn out all right in the end." She nodded. "That's your plan for another night. Let's get their party out of the way tonight."

So they sat down to wait for their hero and bard.

They waited.

Helen looked at her watch. "It's not eleven o'clock yet."

Sapphire described her favourite jewellery to them all.

Lee and Lavender had a colourful conversation about silk, velvet and shoes.

Helen kept checking her watch. It still wasn't eleven o'clock.

They waited.

Sapphire and Sylvie exchanged theories about the best way to eat sheep without getting the wool caught in your teeth.

Yann and Helen chatted about how long it would take for his dad to calm down, and when it would be safe for Yann to go home.

Helen kept checking her watch. "It's eleven o'clock."

They waited.

"It's five past."

"Remember, Ossian doesn't have a watch," Lee pointed out. "He might be running late."

No one was chatting now.

They kept waiting.

They weren't sitting down any more. They were pacing along the ridge, looking along the track for the minibus.

"Ossian has to get here before the students do!" Helen said anxiously. "It's quarter past eleven. He's late."

"He's not late," said Sylvie. "He's not coming. He's let you down." There was a tiny purr of pleasure in her voice.

"He wouldn't let us down. He gave us his word!"

Then Helen's whole body went cold. "Oh no. He did promise. He gave us his solemn word. And he did mean it. But he lives on Tir nan Og. Where the price of eternal life is your memory!"

She groaned, her failure suddenly clear.

"He promised ... and he meant it ... *but he forgot!* He's forgotten his promise. He isn't coming."

There was a deep silence. It was so obvious. How could they not have realized?

Helen groaned again. "Even if Sapphire flies to Fladda-chuain to get him tonight, even if she could find Tir nan Og without a sunset to fly into, he'll have forgotten the tasks we did to win his favour. We would have to do them all again. We don't have time to hunt and fight and riddle again.

"We failed after all. We have no bard. We have no music to provide. Not unless I do it myself."

Helen looked down the ridge. She flinched as minibus headlights suddenly shone along the track.

"I have to get to the mound before the rest of the summer school get here."

"No!" shouted the fabled beasts gathered round her.

"I have to. If I don't, James is trapped there forever. I promised his little sister ..." She forced the words past the panic in her throat. "I promised his little sister he would wake up tonight."

She saw Sylvie sidle over to Yann and whisper. Yann glanced at Helen's fiddle case on the stump.

Helen rushed over, and slung her fiddle on her back.

"Don't you dare, Yann Smith. You are not sabotaging my fiddle any more than you sabotaged the music school. Don't you lay one hoof on this."

He walked towards her slowly. Every hoof beat clear on the hard ground. "I will not let you go in there."

"Yes, you will. You'll let me go in, you'll watch the boy come out and you'll take him home to his family. You will do that."

Helen turned away from Yann, to look at the headlights getting closer.

Sylvie was blocking her view. "You will not go. We will not let you."

"We, Sylvie? You and who else? Are your sneaking skulking spying brothers nearby?"

"Yes. In the forest below the ridge. Just waiting for my word, ready to stop the party."

"But they can't stop it yet. They can't! We haven't got James."

"You aren't going to get him. You have to break your promises, girl. You have to break your promise to the

Queen to provide music, and you have to break your promise to the child to get her brother back."

"I'm not breaking any more promises. I'm not failing any more quests."

Sylvie shook her head, her long silver hair floating in the grey air. "If you aren't going to break your promises, I'm going to keep mine. My promise to the pack. I have held my brothers back from attacking you all week, but I promised I would let them loose when your plans finally fell apart. I will go to my brothers and we will stop this concert."

Sylvie turned and ran, flickering as she went, calling and howling, her voice distorting as her body shifted.

Helen leant against Sapphire, who rumbled comfortingly. Lavender, Lee and Yann gathered round.

"I have failed, haven't I? Right from the start."

She stood up straight. "But your King, Lee ... he said I should finish this quest the way I began and it would all end happily. So let's keep on failing."

"What?" said Lee.

"I've got to keep on *failing*. That's what I have been doing all week. I've got to make a total, utter, complete mess of this.

"But first let's get to the students before the wolves do."

She started to run downhill towards the end of the track.

As she ran, she tried to think of the right words to persuade Sylvie that she finally had a workable plan, and the right words to persuade the other musicians to play along.

She saw the minibus stop, and the inside lights flare as the doors opened.

Everyone jumped out, all dressed in white shirts, dark skirts and dark trousers. Helen groaned once more. She was wearing her mankiest jeans again. She wasn't getting anything right this week.

She wasn't running now, she was creeping, trying to be quiet.

She saw Dr Lermontov's heavy body squeeze out of the driver's door. "Stay where I can see you. We are to wait here until the Professor's front of house staff come to guide us to the venue."

She heard a boy's voice say, "How will we see to play? It's so dark here without streetlights."

Someone else made a wavering ghosty "Oooh Ahahahaha!"

A girl's voice said, "Dark forests are *really creepy* ... "

The same ghosty voice challenged, "I dare you to go in!"

"Don't be daft, that's how horror movies start," the girl laughed. "Some idiot going into the forest on their own."

A fiddler started to play slow eerie music.

There was laughter. "See! Never go into the forest when there's spooky music playing. Everyone knows that!"

Helen, sliding down to the foot of the ridge, heard a howl behind her.

She leapt up and yelled, "Get back in the bus! The Professor says the arriving audience aren't to see you! Get back in the bus!"

There was a confused scramble as people climbed back in and slammed the doors. Dr Lermontov looked round, then hauled himself back into the driver's seat.

Helen called to her friends over the noise of the doors closing. "We have to get between the wolves and the bus."

She heard Yann's hooves thudding on the ground, and saw the bulk of Sapphire flying overhead.

"But don't let the students see you!"

Helen reached the minibus at a sprint, then stumbled back out of the light cast by the bright windows, and stood in the shadows near the rear of the bus.

Yann ordered in a low carrying voice, "Helen, stay there. Lee, to the other back corner. Sapphire, block the path to the forest. I will take the front. Lavender, stay safe on the roof of the bus."

Helen glanced round. "Can the people in the minibus see us?" She really meant, can they see a dragon and a centaur?

"No," answered Yann calmly. "They are in brightness and we are in darkness; if we stay on the edge of the light they won't see us. But we'll keep our fire and glamour and light balls dark, if you don't want them to know we're protecting them."

"Can they hear us?"

"Are you kidding? Listen."

Helen calmed her breathing and listened. The students were playing theme tunes of horror films. Helen smiled.

Lee called, "Helen, do you have a weapon?"

"Of course I don't have a weapon. You're the only one with a weapon, Lee."

"No, Helen. Sapphire has fire, Yann has hooves, the wolves have teeth. We all have weapons except you. Here."

Something rattled at her feet, and Helen bent down

to pick it up. She could feel the shape of the hilt. "This is *your* sword, Lee. Now you've nothing to defend yourself with."

"That's my old sword. The one I damaged last night. I won a new sword today, but even though that old one won't win any more duels, it could still hurt a wolf. Don't be afraid to use it."

Helen stood with the sword heavy in her hand and waited for the wolves.

Chapter 22

It was hard to tell when the wolves arrived.

Helen couldn't see them, she couldn't hear them, but the hair on the back of her neck bristled, and her skin felt cold.

"Sylvie?"

There was no answer. But she was sure they were there.

She couldn't see her enemies. She couldn't see her friends. Just darkness in front of her and yellow light behind. She couldn't step into the light with a sword in her hand. She must not let the wolves past either.

"Sylvie?"

Then she saw, ahead of her, a shining nose and a black muzzle, pushing at the edge of the darkness.

"Yann! Lee! They're here! At my corner of the bus!"

Another long muzzle and huge paws, inching towards her.

Yann called back, "They're here too, Helen. Use the sword!"

Helen lifted the sword. She looked at the advancing wolves.

But what if one of them was Sylvie? She didn't want to hurt Sylvie.

She didn't really want to hurt Sylvie's brothers either. She would rather bandage animals than injure them.

She didn't want to hurt them, but it looked like they wanted to hurt her.

The first wolf, its muzzle getting nearer, bared its teeth and wrinkled its nose, snarling silently at her. It was big, and dark-furred. It definitely wasn't Sylvie.

Helen blew the hair off her face. What should she use? The edge or the point of the sword?

The wolf got nearer. Helen could hardly make out its night-dark back as it slinked towards her. She lifted the sword and crashed it down.

The sword missed the wolf and hit the ground, jarring her wrist.

There was movement to her left. She heard Lee's sword whistle efficiently through the air.

There was movement to her right. There was no one to defend her there. She slashed out again with the sword.

She didn't hit anything, and the wolves, four or five of them now, kept coming towards her. Probably they could see she was the weak point in the defence. She had to look serious with this weapon; she had to feel serious.

Helen gritted her teeth and lunged forward. The wolves all slid backwards.

Then they rushed forward together. She swung the sword in an unwieldy circle. The wolves slowed down, but kept advancing.

This time she jabbed the sword forward, and caught one on the nose. The wolf snarled and leapt back.

"Sylvie! Sylvie!"

She could hear more sword swipes from Lee's corner, and the drumming of hooves on the ground at the front of the minibus. Past the strains of nervewracking horror music from the bus, she could even hear the fizzle of sparks from Sapphire's nostrils. All around, she heard snarls and whines, as her friends beat the wolves back.

But no one howled and no one shouted. No one threw fire or swirled light. They fought quietly in the dark, so those they were protecting didn't even know they were there.

Helen felt the hot breath of the wolves getting nearer.

She jabbed again, then whirled the sword in a fast arc.

Behind the wolves threatening her, she could see, very dimly, more low-slung shapes. More wolves, circling, like sharks round a shipwreck.

"How long can we hold them off?" she panted.

"Until the Queen's guard come to take the musicians to the mound?" asked Lee.

"That'll be too late!" gasped Helen. "I need to talk to the students *before* the faeries get here, or my plan won't work. We need Sylvie. She's the only one who'll understand." Helen swung the sword again, and peered into the gloom. Which slinking shape was Sylvie?

"Sylvie?"

She lowered the sword.

"Sylvie, answer me!"

Lavender's voice called urgently, "Helen! To your right!"

A wolf was sneaking towards the doors of the minibus.

Helen raised the sword and drove it towards the wolf without thinking. There was a moment's dull contact, then a whine. The wolf ran off.

Helen felt sick.

"Sylvie! *Sylvie!* Listen to me!"

"Sylvie isn't with you any more," said a deep voice. "She has shifted. She is with us now."

The darkest wolf had flickered into a tall boy, dressed in elegant black.

"Who are you?" Helen asked almost calmly, much keener to talk than wave a sword about.

"I am Sylvie's big brother and I am here to drive you away. All of you. First the musicians, then the faeries." He took a step towards her.

Helen lifted the heavy sword and pointed it at him. The first time she had pointed it at a person. It wobbled in her hand. "Don't come any closer."

He looked at the sword and smiled cynically. "You're more afraid of that sword than I am! It's useless in your hands."

He looked over her shoulder at the laughing students squashed in the minibus, and grinned more widely. "Like baby rabbits in a burrow. Easy prey, trapped in a small space."

"How are you going to drive them away?" Helen wanted to keep him talking.

"Faeries can't dance to slashed pipes, splintered fiddles, ripped drums and bent flutes. Children can't play with bitten fingers and mangled hands. I will use my teeth and my claws to kill your concert."

He walked forward.

Helen swung the sword at him clumsily.

"Sylvie!" she called again. "Sylvie! I have a plan!"

In the circling pack, a wolf laughed.

"Sylvie, please listen to my plan!"

"Sylvie is not listening to you." The boy took another step. "Now, human girl. Which hand do you play with?" He licked his lips. "Which hand do I bite to stop you playing ever again?"

"I need both my hands to drive the faeries away."

He raised his black eyebrows.

"I need both my hands, and all those hands in the minibus, to drive them away forever.

"If you send us away, scared and bleeding, the faeries will just find more musicians. You know they will. You can't injure every fiddler in Scotland, not without someone noticing.

"But if I drive the faeries away completely, then you can enjoy your forest again.

"Sylvie! Listen to my plan!"

Yann's voice came breathless from the other side of the bus. "Helen, just tell everyone your plan! Sylvie's listening, even if she isn't answering."

"Alright. This is what we do. The wolves back off and let me talk to the students, then we get safely out of the bus and into the mound, and James leaves the mound."

"No. I will let none of that happen." Sylvie's brother smiled with all his long white teeth and shook his shaggy dark head.

"Yes," Helen insisted. "You let us in, and him out. Then we fail."

"You what?"

"We fail. Just like we have all along. Sylvie will understand."

"How do you fail?"

"We play really badly. We embarrass the Queen, we annoy her guests, we drive them away ... with dreadful music. If they're the best audience in the world, then they must hate bad music as much as they love good music. The Professor even said they would leave the revels if we didn't make a good impression."

"I like it," said Lee, who was breathing lightly in the welcome break as everyone round the bus listened to Helen. "Faeries are an audience worth playing to for a hundred years, because we are so sensitive to good music. But we are just as sensitive to bad music. Her plan could work. Let her do it, fur-boy."

The wolf boy snarled.

"I don't like it," called Yann. "How do you get out?"

"We use iron to stop the door closing behind us, and when the faeries leave in disgust, so do we."

"No," said the wolf brother, stalking towards her. Running his long fingers though his black hair, pulling it forward over his forehead and cheeks. "No musician goes in there tonight. Not with all their fingers and ears." He began to flicker.

"No!" said Sylvie suddenly, walking into the dim edge of the light. "The human girl could be right. If we drive away these few musicians, the Queen will find more; if we humiliate her and drive away her guests, she won't come back for years. Let the human girl try."

But the wolf was on all fours now, stalking low to the ground, towards Helen.

Helen couldn't back off, she'd fall into the bright light round the minibus, and it seemed very important to keep this terror private. So she stood still and tried to hold her gaze steady on his green eyes.

He moved closer, and lower.

Then Sylvie leapt on her brother. She knocked him to the ground as a girl, but by the time she got her teeth round his muzzle, she was a wolf.

They wrestled for a moment, then both leapt up. They stood stiff-legged, ears up and hackles bristling, with their two tails, one silver, one black, curled right over their backs. They stared at each other, battling silently and unmoving for dominance. Sylvie was much smaller than her brother, but she refused to cringe to the ground in front of him.

Helen took her chance. She spoke to the darkness, to the rest of the pack. "Sylvie supports me. Listen to your sister. Let me talk to the musicians and tell them how to defeat the Faery Queen.

"While I talk to them, you keep to the shadows. If you scare them, it will be harder to control them."

"Like sheep or deer, you mean?" the wolf boy sneered, as he flickered back up onto his human legs, still glaring at his sister.

"No. Like ordinary people, who don't expect to find wolves or faeries or dragons on their doorsteps."

She stared at him, waiting for his agreement. He licked his lips, then nodded.

Helen moved into the light, and opened the door of the minibus.

She climbed in, closed the door, then realized she was still holding a sword. She pushed it hastily under a seat, with a familiar jarring clang.

"Was that a playground joke, primary girl?" Zoe said. "Trapping us all in this smelly bus while you wander about outside?"

Helen shook her head. "The Professor's venue staff are on their way. We're nearly ready.

"First, I have a message from the Professor. Tonight, she wants us to play our absolute worst."

"What?" a dozen voices asked in surprise.

"She knows we can play well, so tonight, she wants us to play our worst."

"Why?"

Helen took a deep breath.

"She has a theory. Anyone can play music badly. If I picked up your flute, Juliet, I could miss notes, fumble a melody, play out of tune, and it would be bad, but it would be unspectacular and uninteresting. The Professor has a theory that the best players can play the absolute worst. If we put our musical minds to it, we can play really badly; painfully and ear-rattlingly badly. So she wants us to play our worst this evening."

Helen thought she'd explained her plan convincingly and persuasively, but from the shocked faces and shaking heads around her, it was clear she had failed.

"She can't have meant that."

"You must have misunderstood, Helen."

"She wants us to play our best, not our worst, primary girl."

"We can't throw away all that rehearsing!"

Some of them started to get off their seats, picking up their instrument cases.

Helen rubbed her hands nervously on her dusty old jeans. What else could she do?

Then she remembered what was in the pocket of these jeans.

She half stood up, so she could fit her fingers into the tiny pocket, and pulled out the one remaining thread of the Fairy Flag.

She looked at it. Pale and very fragile, it had worked, briefly, on her eyes. Did it have any other powers?

She opened her mouth and laid the thread on her tongue.

She felt an immediate fizzing behind her teeth.

She spoke again. "You are the best musicians the Professor has ever heard."

Her voice rolled round her mouth, it bounced round her skull, it echoed round the minibus. All the students turned to look at her.

"You are the only musicians she would challenge to do this."

Everyone sat down, eyes wide, mouths closed, listening to Helen's voice.

"You are the only musicians she would trust to give their best skills to playing the worst music ever."

They were nodding, smiling.

All except Zoe at the back, who was frowning, and struggling to speak. "No. Just because you didn't get to play a solo … you don't get to ruin it for the rest of us.

"Dr Lermontov," Zoe appealed in a faint voice, "Dr Lermontov, you won't let her do this, will you?"

Helen turned round, to see a puzzled Dr Lermontov

in the driver's seat, pulling a furry hat down over his ears.

He looked hard at Helen, and at the bus full of smiling students. "I'm not sure. But I do know that I heard noises tonight, just before we got back in the bus, which I haven't heard since my childhood in Russia. I remember that my grandmother believed if strange little people give you strange advice on the edge of the forest, it is wise to follow it. So I think we will indeed see how badly we can play. I shall conduct you in the worst concert of our lives!"

The rest of the bus cheered, but Zoe still shook her head.

Helen ran her tongue over the roof of her mouth, and aimed a warm stream of words at the back of the bus. "Zoe, you can play a solo if you like. Improvise your own answer to the Professor's challenge."

Zoe smiled and nodded, slowly.

Helen grinned. "We can all come up with our own ways to play the worst music ever. The Professor is interested in our original ideas. She will be listening very carefully!"

"We could all play different tunes at once," suggested Alice.

"We could use different tempos, starting and finishing separately," offered Amelia.

"Or play a tune backwards?" Catriona wondered.

There were giggles at that suggestion, then lots more students started having ideas.

"Play in the style of an old man farting, or a baby burping," Tommy laughed.

"Or play your wolf note, Helen," offered Juliet.

"Yes! Play the notes you know your instrument hates," agreed Zoe.

Now everyone was laughing, and everyone had ideas of the best ways to play horrible music. All shouting out at once.

Helen sighed in relief. The students might be enchanted, but at least they were having fun …

She swallowed the fizzing taste in her mouth, opened the door, and said loudly, "Let's go and do our worst!"

She felt the night air lifted by a sigh of relief, and heard feet, hooves, claws and paws moving back into the dark.

As everyone got out of the minibus and took their instruments out of their cases, tall cloaked figures came out of the forest, with high torches flaming above them.

"Front of house?" enquired Dr Lermontov.

Helen watched as the summer school students filed after the torch-bearing faeries. Then she reached into the minibus, to pull out the sword and the spanner it had clanged against. She had recognised the sound of bronze hitting iron.

She whispered into the darkness as she followed the line of torches, "Bye, Sapphire. I'll be back out before your tail grows longer or your fire burns hotter."

Then she spoke to the silvery figure walking on her left.

"Sylvie, the wolves I hurt with the sword. Do they need any first aid?"

"We have our own healers. You have done enough to them."

There was an awkward silence.

Helen spoke again. "Thanks for trusting me and for saving me from your brother."

236

Sylvie growled. "Now repay that trust and drive the faeries away, or my brothers will never listen to another word I say!" She faded into the darkness.

There was a swish of scented velvet to Helen's right.

"Lee. Here's your sword back. I didn't really like using it."

"You wielded it well, Helen, and you will wield your bow well in there too. I'm sure your plan will work. I trust you. And thank you for trusting me, when no one else did."

The velvet swirled away, but Helen heard a whisper, "Please remember, you'd be foolish to trust me any other time …"

Then Helen felt a light touch on her shoulder.

"Bye, Lavender. See you soon."

"I'm coming in with you, Helen. Sitting on your shoulder, as usual."

Helen laughed nervously. "You can't sit on my shoulder when I'm playing. If you sit on my left shoulder, I'll crush you with the fiddle; if you sit on my right shoulder, I'll jerk you off as I move my bow arm. And if the Faery Queen saw you, she would eat you up like a party snack! Stay out here and wait for me. I won't be long. I promise. You know I try to keep my promises."

Lavender flew off her shoulder, whispering, "Please be careful, Helen."

Then she felt the sudden warm bulk of Yann overtaking her.

"I wish I was coming in with you, Helen."

"You can't, Yann. I have to do this task all on my own. You will take James home safely, won't you? If I know

I can trust you with that, then I can concentrate on getting everyone else out."

"Of course you can trust me."

"I know that," she said. "I've always known that."

She walked away from her friends towards the long dark hump of the faery mound.

The tall torch bearers stood by the hill, a wide arch opened and golden light flooded out.

Everyone else stepped in confidently and happily, with no idea of where they were heading. Helen hesitated. If she walked in, would she ever walk out again?

She waited in the shadows until even the torch bearers were inside. As she stepped into the mound, she punched the spanner into the side of the arch. Then she walked into the Faery Queen's midsummer revels.

Chapter 23

Helen walked into a huge feasting hall.

The students ahead of her were staring at the room. The domed ceiling was hung with huge circles of wood, candles burning on their upper rims. The walls were decorated with tapestries of hunts, feasts and dances, framed by bone-white antlers and embossed bronze shields.

The students looked hungrily at tables covered in ashets of roast meat, poached fruit, honeycombs and warm bread, jugs of ale and steaming cogs of mead.

Helen thought she'd better get them playing before they were tempted to eat anything.

Then she noticed the guests. As the students stared at the faery splendour, the guests at the revels stared just as hard at their musical entertainment. Their shining cloaks flung over chairs and stools, their smooth skin pale in the candlelight, their beautiful faces gazing in wonder at the young musicians in the centre of the hall.

Helen looked at the audience. Where was the Professor?

She couldn't see her, but she could see so many other welcoming enthusiastic faces. Hands applauding encouragingly as the summer school students got their instruments ready.

Suddenly Helen wondered what harm it could do to play properly *first*. Surely they could show their skills first, then do the appalling music later, to drive the faeries away at the end. Then the faeries would know what they were missing, and Helen could hear, the students could hear, the applause and encores they deserved.

Helen smiled at the audience, and tapped her toes on the floor, in the rhythm of the Professor's music. The faeries began to clap along. Helen pulled her fiddle case off her shoulders. If the Professor wasn't here, the Professor couldn't stop her playing a solo, just a quick one, all on her own.

Then she heard a voice. "Are you the sandwich lady?"

She spun round, and saw a small boy at the end of the hall, sitting below two tall golden thrones. Both thrones were covered with feathery canopies, thatched with wings of all colours: blue, red, yellow, white, purple.

Helen moved closer. She recognized the overlapping arrangement of the feathers. They weren't bird wings. They were flower fairy wings.

These faeries decorated their thrones with flower fairy wings!

Helen swallowed the sour taste in her mouth and put her fiddle away. They didn't deserve her music. She must drive these faeries away, before their cruelty spread further through the forest.

She looked down from the canopies to the people seated on the thrones. She saw the Faery King's stern face, asking a question with his raised eyebrows. Helen nodded, once. He smiled.

Then she looked straight at the Faery Queen, seeing her for the first time without a veil of distance.

The Queen, dressed in pure radiant white, held out her slim hands. "Helen. You have provided music for me. How kind. You may start now."

"Not yet."

Helen looked down at the floor below the Queen's throne. There was James, sitting on a cushion, pale, grubby and bleary.

"Come on, James. Time to go home."

"What a shame," crooned the Queen. "Do let him stay for just one tune."

"No," said Helen. "No music until he has gone. Bedtime, James. Off you go. My friend Yann will take you home. Go home and give Emma a cuddle."

James stood up and repeated, "Are you the sandwich lady?"

Helen grinned. "Yes. Did you like them?"

"Not really. I like sandwiches with crusts, they're chewier." He trotted across the hall, towards the arched exit.

Helen shook her head. Even her picnics had been a failure this week.

Then she stared in surprise at the Queen. Now that James had moved away, Helen could see the Queen's feet for the first time. Her pointy, stiletto shoes; bright white with gold heels, perfectly polished and free of dust.

At last, Helen realized that the Faery Queen had organized the summer school herself. She had written the music for her revels with her own fair hands. Of course.

"Hello, Professor," she said to the Queen.

"Hello, Helen," the Queen answered. "Aren't you slow to catch on? Time for my revels. We are all waiting."

"I hope you think it's worth waiting for."

Helen grabbed her fiddle and joined the huddle of musicians.

She heard the pulse of hoof beats outside and grinned. James was going home.

Then she licked her lips. Her tongue was no longer fizzing. Her words would have no special power. Would the musicians still agree to play their worst?

"Remember ..." she whispered. "Play your wolf notes. Your sharps and flats. Play backwards. And whatever you do, don't play along with the person next to you. Do your worst! And have fun!"

They all nodded, as sure as they had been when they left the bus that this was what the Professor wanted them to do, what they wanted to do.

So when Dr Lermontov lifted his baton, everyone played a note. Not one of them played the note the music was meant to begin with, but very few had the courage to play a second note after it, and no one played a third note. There was a pause. How could you play out of tune and out of time with everyone else, when you didn't know what they were going to play next?

He waved again, and everyone played another note,

but several of them actually harmonized, completely by accident.

Helen gasped. Failing was harder than she thought. Particularly when you were trying to fail.

So she grasped her bow firmly and started to play into the silence. She played "Pop goes the Weasel."

She heard a giggle, and someone next to her started "Humpty Dumpty," then a drummer started banging out "A Shave and a Haircut". A flautist played "Mary Mary Quite Contrary" in a gratingly minor key, and Zoe laughed and played "Jack and Jill" purely on harmonics.

Suddenly they were all picking a different simple tune and playing it again and again, fast and slow, sharp and flat, loud and soft, minor and major, mangling it and murdering it, and it sounded …

Awful!

Helen lifted her head for a moment to look at the audience.

Their gleaming white faces were turning green.

They had their hands clasped to their ears.

They were screaming silently.

Once the bagpipers found their true volume and started playing tunes from *Mary Poppins* backwards, the faeries started to leave. They held each other up, swaying and wobbling, then they fled, pushing aside the golden tapestries and slipping into the dark tunnels hidden behind them.

"Keep it up," yelled Helen, switching to the duck-swallowing music from *Peter and the Wolf*.

Some hardier faeries, with caps pulled down over their ears, were throwing food and drink towards the musicians, trying to shut them up. But the food turned into bunches of grass and handfuls of nuts as it flew through the air, and the ale and mead became raindrops, drizzling onto their heads.

The students laughed, playing louder and faster, and the food-throwing faeries gagged and fled.

The King and Queen were still there, surrounded by an angry group of guests pulling their cloaks up round their ears.

So Helen looked up at the ceiling and, judging the acoustics as she stepped forward, she started to play her wolf note. The note she avoided as much as she could, the note which set up such a vibration in the fiddle that it was hard to keep the bow on the string.

The wolf note howled wildly round the room. Helen played it again and again and again, and as she stood under the centre of the dome, the echoes crashed round the hall, torturing the air.

The last of the faery guests, moaning with pain, slid out round a tapestry of a hound bringing down a deer.

"March out, but keep playing," Helen yelled, so Tommy led the way, beating a stuttering mix of salsa and waltz on his bodhran that made everyone trip over each other's feet.

Helen finally stopped playing her screaming wolf note, and joined the end of the procession, turning back to look at the thrones.

The Queen was shrieking, her face red, her hair falling out of its bun, just as it always had in lessons. "How dare you! How dare you ruin my revels!"

"I promised I would provide music," Helen shouted back. "I didn't promise it would be any good!"

She glanced at the King, who had his golden cloak stuffed into his ears. He gave her a cheerful wink.

Then she noticed Lee, standing in the shadow behind his King, staring at her hands on her fiddle with the same glittering hunger she had seen when she whistled in the forest.

Lee looked up to her face and smiled, as brightly and beautifully as ever. He held out a hand to her. Helen shook her head, then ran through the arched doorway, pulling the spanner from the earth as she passed.

The door clanged shut behind her; a hollow echo, as if the mound was already empty … and would stay empty for a hundred years.

Helen tripped over a heap of musicians lying on the black midnight grass, laughing.

"I hope someone was recording that!"

"It was horrible!"

"I sounded appalling! Worse than a six-year-old learning the chanter!"

"That was so much fun!"

"Do you think the Professor will write a paper on it? Will she mention our names?"

Over the giggles, Helen heard hoof beats getting closer and, in the distance, triumphant howls.

She raised her voice. "Shall we play properly now? To prove that we really are the best musicians in Scotland!"

"Who would we be playing for?" asked Zoe.

"For ourselves," said Helen, "and for anyone listening in the forest."

"There's no one listening in the forest."

Helen just grinned, and put her fiddle to her shoulder.

And they played.

They played Professor Fay Greenhill's magical music, at midnight on midsummer night, to anyone listening in the forest.

Only Helen knew who was listening.

Only Helen heard the whispers of "encore" in that moment of silence when the music finally stopped.

Read on for a sneak preview of
Helen's next adventure in

Storm Singing
and
Other Tangled Tasks

Yann yelled suddenly, "Rona! Come back!"

"No! I can't be late!"

"Come and look at this!"

"Look at what, the seaweed in your tail?"

"Rona Grey, I'm serious. Come here!"

Rona turned back, glancing up at the sun in the same irritated way Helen's mum checked her watch when she had to get Helen to school, Nicola to nursery and already had animals queuing outside her vet's surgery.

"What?" Rona demanded.

"Look at that sand ..." The centaur pointed between his front hooves.

Both girls stared at a clear patch of sand.

"There's nothing there!" they said at the same time.

"Precisely. There's nothing there. It's completely smooth. Something has been rubbed out."

Helen peered closer. The stretch of sand *was* utterly smooth. She looked at other patches of sand between the rocks. They were marked with bird footprints and the soft lines of the last tide.

Rona knelt down and sniffed. "You're right. No wind-blown grains. No salty crust. Someone has brushed this."

"Someone has covered their traces," insisted Yann. "Someone who doesn't want anyone to know they've been here."

"Who?" asked Rona, her irritation turning to worry.

Yann shrugged. "Someone spying on the Storm Singer competition?"

"But it's a public event. Any sea being or fabled beast is welcome to watch. And humans don't know about it."

"I know about it," said Helen.

"Only because I invited you."

"We can't tell who it is unless we track them," said Yann. "We can't tell what they want unless we ask them." He cracked his knuckles and grinned.

Helen sighed, and Rona shook her head.

"It's a peaceful competition, Yann, not a battle," said Rona. "I'm sure someone brushed the sand for a perfectly sensible reason."

"I'll investigate," announced Yann.

"*You?*" snorted Rona. "*You* are struggling to walk in a straight line on this beach. I suppose I'd better go." She looked at the sun again.

"You can't go," said Yann. "You only get one chance to enter the Storm Singer competition, Rona, and if you win that, it's your only chance to become Sea Herald. You can't be late. I'll go."

"No," said Helen. "I'll go. You two get to the competition at your own speeds, and I'll check out this possible spy."

"If you find a spy, Helen, what will you do?" demanded Yann. "If you find a kraken or blue man, a sea kelpie or sea serpent, a nuckelavee or giant eel, what will you do?"

Helen frowned at Yann's scary list, then shrugged. "See if they need a plaster? Play them a solo on my fiddle?" She patted the violin case on her back.

"Don't joke, human girl. The edge where sea and land meet may be a holiday destination to you, but like any joining of two worlds, it draws evil beings from both."

Helen grinned. "I've dealt with a power-hungry minotaur and a child-stealing Faery Queen in the last year. I can sneak up on a seaside spy."

Rona wailed, "But if *you* go, Helen, you won't hear me sing!"

"Yes, I will. Your volume and confidence have improved so much in the last two days, I'd hear you even if I was still in Taltomie."

Rona blushed. "Do you think so? If I'm louder and more confident, it's because of your coaching. You're much better at performing than me."

"You write better music, so it evens out. Now get going, and I'll track down your mystery guest. I'll probably be in the audience in time for your songs, and if not, just project loudly enough to reach me wherever I am. Good luck!"

They hugged, and Rona smiled. "I'll get to Geodha Oran faster without you two anyway."

She ran down to the sea's edge, pulled her furry rucksack off, flapped it open, and swung the sealskin cloak over her shoulders. She shimmered in the sunlight reflecting off the sea, crouched on the rocks, then bounced into the water.

A seal.

She waved a fin, and swam off.

Helen turned to Yann. "You carry on along the seaweed, while I go on this wild-goose chase."

"If it's something as small as a wild goose that's

been covering its tracks, I'll be delighted. Anyway, I'm coming with you."

"You're as wobbly as a newborn foal on these rocks. What use will you be?"

"The creature isn't on these rocks. The patches of cleared sand lead up the beach, towards that cliff. Even if it isn't doing anything sinister, it seems to be taking an inland route to the venue. So I'll get there faster and safer by following it."

Once Yann had struggled to the base of the cliff, he pointed up the steep rock wall. "A path, with more brush marks. Let's climb up."

Now it was Helen's turn to feel insecure. Yann trotted up the gritty narrow path like a goat, while Helen concentrated on every step.

When they got near the top, Helen whispered, "I'll peek over, I'm smaller and quieter than you."

She edged past Yann and saw an expanse of pale salt-blown grass, with grey rocks scattered along the cliff edge as if they'd been tossed there by storms. "It's clear. Nothing here."

Yann stepped up, and checked the landscape carefully, just in case Helen had missed a sea monster right in front of her. He nodded. "It's clear, and I can't see any tracks on this grass. Let's go towards Geodha Oran. If this creature is watching the contest, we'll spot it on the way."

As they followed the jutting and jagged coastline, Helen asked, "What's a Sea Herald?"

"Pardon?"

"I thought Rona was competing in the selkies' Storm Singer competition, but you said this was her only chance to become a Sea Herald. What did you mean?"

"Hasn't she told you, all those mornings you've spent screeching on the beach?"

Helen shook her head, and Yann smiled down at her, like he always did when he explained something Helen didn't know.

"This afternoon's competition, ignorant human child, is just for selkies competing to become a Storm Singer, the highest level of sea singer. Today's victor then enters a contest between selkies and other sea tribes, to become Sea Herald. Hardly any Storm Singers get the chance to be Sea Herald, because these contests are held very rarely, so Rona is under a lot of pressure to win.

"Her mum and two cousins are Storm Singers. Her great-grandmother was a Sea Herald. Rona has a family reputation to uphold. Maybe that's why she didn't tell you, in case it made you both nervous."

Helen frowned. "She did say it was a family tradition to win the Storm Singer competition. She's wearing the dress her mum wore when she won. But she didn't say that if she wins she'll have to enter another competition! I don't know if I can coach her through more songs. She gets so *anxious*!"

"You won't have to. The Sea Herald contest isn't a performance, it's a race and a quest. If she becomes a Storm Singer with your help, she'll need my help to become Sea Herald."

"Rona? In a race and a quest? You're kidding!"

Helen wished she hadn't given Rona so much advice on performing. Perhaps Rona would be happier if she didn't win this competition, then she wouldn't have to endure another one.

But Rona's greatest pleasure was to write and sing

songs, and the winning Storm Singer was invited to sing at lots of fabled beast gatherings.

Then Helen heard distant voices and faint laughter.

"We're nearly there," said Yann. "Let's find a place we can watch as well as listen."

"What about the ...?"

Suddenly they both saw it.

A rock, on the cliff edge.

A pool of shadow behind the rock.

A shape, shifting, in the shadow.

Helen and Yann stopped.

The figure moved round the rock, peered down at the crowd below, and the bright afternoon sunlight touched its head.

Helen and Yann gasped.

To be continued ...

TIME TRAVEL TROUBLE

from Scottish Children's Book Award winner Janis Mackay

Time travel is a tricky business. From getting a lost girl back to *when* she came from, to finding lost title deeds when the world is on the verge of war, Saul and Agnes's time-twisting adventures could lead to a whole host of problems…

Lewis and Greg might have *accidentally* summoned Loki, the Norse god of mischief. Not to mention his hammer-wielding big brother Thor, who's trapped in the boys' garage... But it wasn't their fault!

With a gang of valkyries chasing them from St Andrews to Asgard, can the troublesome twosome outwit Loki and save the day?

Mischievous fairies? Smelly troll? Werewolf snatching your sheep? Email the Really Weird Removals company!

Luca and Valentina's Uncle Alistair runs a pest control business. But he's not getting rid of rats. The Really Weird Removals Company catches supernatural creatures! When the children join Alistair's team they befriend a lonely ghost, rescue a stranded sea serpent, and trap a cat-eating troll.